GUNHAWK
HARVEST

GUNHAWK HARVEST

Leslie Ernenwein

Thorndike Press • Waterville, Maine

Published in 2003 by arrangement with Golden West Literary
Agency.

Thorndike Press Large Print Paperback Series.

The tree indicium is a trademark of Thorndike Press.

The text of this Large Print edition is unabridged.
Other aspects of the book may vary from the original edition.

Set in 16 pt. Plantin.

Printed in the United States on permanent paper.

ISBN 0-7862-4941-2 (lg. print : sc : alk. paper)

To
BETTY JANTZ
*In memory of the Westerlo Hills
away back yonder and a long time ago*

AUTHOR'S NOTE

Although this story is based on historical happenings in Arizona's dramatic past, the continuity of events has been purposely adjusted to suit the needs of plot. All characters herein mentioned, with the exception of Rangers Tom Rynning, Burt Mossman, Jeff Kidder, Billy Olds and Timberline Sparks, are fictional. If the name of any other actual person has been used it is coincidental, and was not included in the vast amount of source material, written and oral, which furnished the basic ingredients of this novel.

LESLIE ERNENWEIN

Tucson

CONTENTS

CHAPTER 1

In a Dead Man's Saddle

Sundown's long shadows were cloaking the east slope of Mormon Ridge when Lee Ransome unsaddled his roan gelding. Far behind him were Maricopa Wells, Oatman's Flat and Telegraph Pass. Ahead of him, obscured by autumn haze, lay Concho Basin and his last gamble with guns.

Lee Ransome was thinking about that as he kindled a fire for the battered coffeepot and small skillet which comprised his cooking utensils. This was what five years of gunhawking had brought him — a lonely campfire in the brush and a chance to die with his boots on. For that was what this final, fantastic deal added up to, unless he was uncommon lucky.

A cynical smile creased Ransome's whisker-shagged cheeks. According to his philosophy a man rated only so much luck in one lifetime. Rich or poor, smart or dim-witted, he got about the same treatment from Lady Luck. She might smile at him continuously for months, or even years; men might call him a lucky son and be envious of his good fortune. But sooner or later there always came a time when the string ran out; when the inevitable adjustment of odds brought the balancing scales to dead center. That time, Ransome thought, was overdue for him. Lady Luck had held her arm around him for five tumultuous years since Texas Junction — since the dismal day he had become a gun-grabbing pariah.

Remembering all the times he might have gone down in gut-shot agony, Ransome mused, "I've been goddam lucky."

But those years had left their claw marks on him, regardless. They had turned his eyes cold and hard and sharp with wariness; bleak with remembering. The smoky years had shaped his angular face to toughness so that he appeared older than his twenty-eight years. And some of the marks, deep inside, didn't show. He made a lonely shape, eating supper there beside his campfire. Against the vast backdrop of Mormon Ridge he was a symbol of isolation and aloneness — a trail-weary wanderer in a wild unfriendly land.

Finishing his frugal meal, Ransome took

a folded sheet of note paper from his pocket and contemplated the sketched map of Concho Basin, observing that Gunman's Camp lay about midway between Gillum's Circle G ranch and Tarborrow's Bootjack, with the town of Tonto Bend to the southeast. He gave the map a lingering appraisal, reckoning the distances between those three locations and thinking of their importance in relation to the task that brought him here. Finally he glanced at the pencil-scrawled message below the map, addressed to Cameo Kimble:

The bearer is Lee Ransome. He got railroaded to Yuma and will make you a good man.
Fred Lomax

It was a lie, of course. Lee Ransome hadn't been railroaded to Yuma. He had gone there of his own accord. But the note might get him into Gunman's Camp; and Fred Lomax, who was serving ten years for rustling, would never know his name had been forged. . . .

"A loco proposition," Ransome muttered, and recalled using those exact words when Tom Rynning first suggested it. But Captain Rynning had said, "You're the one man who might put it over. The feud in Concho Basin has the makings of another Lincoln County War and Sheriff Baffert has passed the buck to me."

Ransome frowned, remembering. He had felt like saying: "No, by God! It's no meat off my rump what happens to Concho Basin!"

He had wanted to tell Rynning that he'd had his fill of fighting — more than aplenty. More than one man should have in a whole lifetime. He had wanted to explain that it had taken five years for the hate to burn out of him, so that he could be as other men. But he couldn't seem to find the right words, nor refuse a favor to a friend. Tom Rynning must've known that, Ransome thought now, and taken full advantage of the knowledge.

Ransome shaped up a smoke. He drew a burning branch from the fire and held it to his cigarette and said again, "A loco proposition."

That was when he heard the drumbeat of hoofs on the ridge above him; a rapidly increasing clatter that became a thunderous rumble as he ran toward his hobbled horse. It was a sound no man who'd ever worked cattle would mistake — the ominous, spine-chilling sound of stampeding cattle!

The first big steers came crashing through the brush almost at Ransome's heels. They hit the camp head-on, running wild through the fire's smouldering embers and stampeding on down the ridge at breakneck speed. Ransome peered through the upchurned dust and smoke, saw that his horse was unhurt, and loosed a gusty sigh. Then, as the stink of a burning blanket came to him, he contemplated the trampled wreckage of his camp and cursed dejectedly. There had probably been no more than twenty steers in that rampaging bunch, but they'd ruined his belongings completely. The saddle was a flattened mass of hoof-tromped leather, its wooden tree smashed and one oxbow stirrup broken to splinters. The tattered remnants of his blanket were afire, and there was no sign of coffeepot or skillet.

"The wall-eyed bastards," Ransome said whisperingly.

It didn't occur to him that he had been lucky to escape with his life; that only the instinctive dash toward his horse had saved him from being trampled to death in that wild rush of cattle. All he saw was a ruined saddle and camp outfit. He was morosely swearing when a rider slid to a halt on the dusk-veiled ridge above him and demanded, "What are you doing there?"

There was something about the voice that seemed odd to Ransome. But resentment was having its way with him and so he called toughly, "What in hell is the idea of stampeding cattle through a man's camp?"

Then, as the rider came close, he understood why the voice had seemed odd to him. The rider was a girl — a tall, dark-haired girl whose hat, hanging by its throat cord, framed a high cheeked face with wide gray eyes. Gray, or blue, he couldn't be sure which; but her lips, parted now by gusty breathing, were the reddest and most expressive lips he'd ever seen.

"My goodness!" she exclaimed, peering at the wreckage. "They must've run right through your camp!"

"Yeah," Ransome agreed sarcastically. "They must've."

Then he asked, "Do you always work your cattle at a dead run, ma'am?"

The girl's full lips curved into a sheepish smile. "They spooked on me," she explained. "I had them trailing pretty as you please when all of a sudden they turned into high-tailing bunch-quitters. I tried to head them north, toward the ranch, but

14

they wouldn't turn."

"Trifle early for beef roundup," Ransome suggested.

The girl shrugged, her gesture expressing a weariness that matched the note of futility in her voice as she said, "It takes cash to run a range war. Cash on the barrelhead."

Then she added, "I'm real sorry about wrecking your camp, Mister —"

"Ransome," he offered. "Lee Ransome."

"And I'm Belle Gillum," she said.

"Big Bart Gillum's daughter?" Ransome inquired.

When she nodded he said, "I've got a bridle around here somewhere, if those steers didn't tote it off with them," and began searching the hoof-gouged ground.

Belle Gillum dismounted and built a fire of broken branches to make some light, then joined in the search. It was fully dark now, with night's coolness coming off the high hills; with night's strict silence broken only by the continued panting of Belle's sweat-lathered horse.

She examined Ransome's smashed saddle, seeing at once that it was ruined beyond repair. "If you'll come to Circle G I'll give you a saddle to replace it," she offered.

That surprised Ransome, for there were seldom extra saddles at a ranch. "How come you've got one to spare?" he inquired.

"It belonged to my Uncle Clem," she said quietly. "He was killed last week."

"So?" Ransome mused, remembering that there had been three Gillum brothers and four Tarborrows when the feud started six months ago. Now there was one Gillum and two Tarborrows. . . .

It took upwards of ten minutes to locate the bridle which had been carried down-slope by a stampeding steer. One bit shank was bent and the reins badly mangled, but the bridle could be used.

Ransome led his horse toward the fire and was strongly conscious of the picture Belle Gillum made standing there. She wasn't more than two or three years past twenty, he judged, but those years had transformed girlish beauty into a woman's full-blown loveliness — had rounded and ripened her so that the cotton shirt and brush-scabbed chaps she wore couldn't conceal the womanly contours of her body.

It was an odd thing. Lee Ransome, who had consistently shrugged off the invitations of honkytonk sirens in seductive silk gowns and ignored the smiles of flirty waitresses wearing peekaboo blouses, was really looking at a girl for the first time in five years. The first time since that tragic day in Texas Junction.

Belle said, "I've been trying to remember where I've seen you before," and her eyes were steadily appraising as Ransome stepped into the circle of firelight.

"You haven't," he said.

"What makes you so sure?"

Ransome grinned, liking her frank friendliness. "Well, if we'd met I wouldn't have forgotten seeing you. And I'd have found out what color your eyes were."

"You should know now," she said censuringly, "the way you've been gawking at me."

But she was smiling when she said it and so Ransome peered at her in mock concern, asking, "Are they blue, or gray, ma'am?"

"That's for you to decide. But I still think I've seen you before, somewhere."

Ransome shook his head. "This is my first visit to Concho Basin," he said. A cynical smile quirked his long lips and he added, "It will also be the last."

He vaulted onto the roan's back, and Belle climbed into saddle, saying, "Concho Basin was a pleasant place to live until the

Tarborrows turned it into a hateful place."

"From what I hear the Gillums have also done some fighting," Ransome suggested slyly.

"That's right, but it was decent fighting," Belle insisted. "Not bushwhacking. The Tarborrows knew there'd be a fight when they brought sheep south of the Rim. That's why they did it. They're cowmen, not sheepherders, but because my father crossed them they brought sheep in to spite him."

"The same old, sorry situation," Ransome mused.

"But it wasn't, really," Belle insisted. "The trouble started before the sheep came in. My father did everything he could to keep it from turning into a range war. He gave orders not to shoot at herders when the first band of sheep came. Nor at the Tarborrows who guarded the sheep. Two bands of sheep were destroyed, and the herders were allowed to go back north of the Rim, where they belonged. But the Tarborrows wouldn't admit they were licked, even then. Instead they started dry-gulching Gillum riders. They turned it into a dog-eat-dog affair, fighting like kill-crazy Apaches. And now Dad is doing the same. He doesn't like it, but that's the way it is."

18

Then she said abruptly, "I know who you reminded me of — Jim Tarborrow. You've got the same dark and hungry look."

Ransome grinned, recalling that a convict named Jim Tarborrow was the pawn in this loco deal. . . .

"He was sent to Yuma Prison for robbing my father in a payroll holdup," Belle explained. "That's what really started all the trouble."

"So I've heard," Ransome said. "Tarborrow claimed he was innocent, didn't he?"

"Of course," she said. "But even though he wore a mask he didn't fool my father. Sheriff Sid Baffert trailed a horse with a broken shoe and found Jim Tarborrow riding it. He told a wild story in court about being forced to swap horses with a masked bandit, but everyone knows he was lying."

Not everyone, Ransome thought. The prison padre at Yuma believed Jim Tarborrow's story — the simple straightforward story the young convict had repeated to Ransome a week ago. And Captain Tom Rynning of the Arizona Rangers was willing to believe Tarborrow had told the truth. Not merely willing, but eager to believe it. His parting prediction had been: "If you can prove Jim Tarborrow wasn't the bandit who held up Big Bart Gillum you'll end the Concho Basin feud *muy pronto*. But there's only one way it can be proved — find the real bandit."

Which was why Lee Ransome, who'd wanted to quit the gun game and go to homesteading, had joined the Arizona Rangers instead. It was what brought him to Concho Basin with a forged note to Cameo Kimble. "He's running what's called Gunman's Camp," Rynning had explained. "That's the logical place to do your looking."

Presently, as Ransome followed Belle Gillum along the dark ridge, she asked, "Were you just riding through, Mister Ransome?"

"Not exactly," Ransome said and, sensing the swift suspicion those words kindled, was remotely amused. Belle Gillum, he guessed, would be wondering why he was here. She'd be wanting to know if he were a Tarborrow recruit.

For a time they rode in silence. This entry into feud-torn Concho Basin was different from what Lee Ransome had planned. Recalling how long a time it had been since he'd associated with a pretty woman, Ransome understood why Belle Gillum disrupted the single-purpose trend of his thinking. She made a man remember better days, and pleasanter ways; a time when moonlight meant romance and there'd been no corroding memories of a dead girl in Texas Junction.

Afterward, as the lights of Circle G appeared in a valley below, Belle said, "I don't like to seem overly inquisitive, Mister Ransome. But my father will want to know what your business is in Concho Basin."

"Maybe I'll tell him it's my business, and none of his," Ransome said.

She halted her horse at once. She said urgently, "Then you'd better not come to the ranch. Big Bart used to be a kind, friendly man. There wasn't a kinder man in all Arizona Territory. But losing two brothers, and all the other trouble, has changed him. He hates the Tarborrows, and everyone connected with them. He might shoot you down like a dog if he even suspects you're on the other side."

"Suppose I told him I was heading for Cameo Kimble's place?" Ransome asked.

He couldn't see her face, but the tone of her voice told him how surprised she was. "So that's it!" she exclaimed. And there was a plain note of disdain when she added, "It didn't occur to me that you were a professional gunhawk. You, well, you don't seem quite that common."

"Never try to tell how hard a bronc will pitch by looking at him," Ransome warned. And because she had admittedly graded him a notch above Kimble's renegades, he felt a queerly warming satisfaction. Then he thought: *Hell, I am a professional gunhawk. Been one for five years.*

He knew then how surprisingly much this association with a warm-eyed, friendly woman had affected him. For a brief interval tonight he had been like he'd used to be, previous to Texas Junction. . . .

Cow smell came faintly across the dark flats as Ransome rode toward Circle G's lamp-lit windows with Belle Gillum. Stars twinkled all across the high arch of a cloudless sky and a soft evening breeze whispered through occasional clumps of mesquite. It seemed almost impossible that this could be bloody Concho Basin where men were forced to take sides in a gunsmoke vendetta, or quit the country; where gunhung men rode warily, even in broad daylight.

Ransome was thinking about that when he heard hooftromp off to the east. An instinctive wariness sent his right hand to holster; he was wholly alert when two riders trotted up, one of them calling anxiously, "Is that you, Belle?"

"Yes, Dad," she said, and lowering her voice to a confidential tone, said to Ransome, "Please mind how you talk to him."

Big Bart Gillum demanded, "Who's that with you?"

"A man named Ransome," she announced. "My gather got away and stampeded through his camp. We owe him a saddle."

The two riders swung into the trail and now Gillum said irritably, "Begun to think you'd got throwed, girl. How many head you lose?"

"Seventeen. The darn critters boogered on me, crossing Mormon Ridge."

Gillum eased in close beside Ransome, making a huge shadow shape in the lesser darkness here. "What was you doin' on the ridge?"

"Camping for the night," Ransome said in a barely civil tone.

Gillum struck a match, holding it cupped so that Ransome's face was briefly revealed in the flare, and his own as well. "Just ridin' through?" he asked.

The flat arrogance of the question kindled a swift resentment in Lee Ransome. It showed in his voice when he said bluntly, "No."

"Then what's your business in Concho Basin?" Gillum demanded.

Belle said quickly, "He's heading for Gunman's Camp."

"Oh," Gillum muttered. They were into the yard now and he peered sharply at Ransome as they passed through the doorway's shaft of lamplight. "So you're one of them."

And the way he said *them,* giving the word a deliberate emphasis, showed what he thought of Cameo Kimble's companions.

The other rider, a beardless youth who looked to be about sixteen, said, "I'll take care of your horse, Miss Belle."

She dismounted, murmuring, "Thanks, Kid."

That casual expression of appreciation seemed to please the young cowpoke immensely. *He's got a case on her,* Ransome thought, and remembering how pleasing a picture she had made beside the campfire, understood that any man who looked at Belle Gillum might get romantic notions. Even a gunsmoke pariah from Texas Junction. . . .

She said, "The saddle is in the wagon shed, Mister Ransome. I'll show you."

Other men were stripping gear from horses over at the corral, their talk reaching across the yard as Ransome walked to the shed with Belle. "Upwards of two hundred fifty head, the way I tally 'em," a rider announced. "You reckon that'll be enough, Bart?"

"Have to be," Gillum replied. "We've got no more time to spend gatherin' 'em."

An old man wearing a flour-sack apron called from the kitchen doorway, "Supper's on and gittin' cold!"

As if in punctuation of that summons a gun blasted somewhere beyond the corral. The cook loosed a croaking curse; he fell against the doorframe with both hands clutching his chest, and Ransome thought fleetingly: *He shouldn't have stood in that lamplight.*

Now, as other guns opened up, a swirling confusion of plunging horses and yelling men broke loose in the yard. Ransome pushed Belle into the shed, heard her exclaim, "Those Tarborrow devils!"

She tried to pull away from him; she cried, "I've got to drag Cookie out of that doorway!"

"You're staying right here," Ransome told her. Clinging to the roan's reins with one hand, he used the other to hold Belle

25

against the shed's wall. When a bullet whanged close, splintering a board, he pressed against her, making a shield of his body. For a brief interval, while the feminine scent of her hair was a delicate perfume for him, Ransome remained hard against her.

The firing ended as abruptly as it had begun. There was an instant of shocked silence followed by a derisive yell and a clatter of hoofbeats, that sound rapidly diminishing. A nuisance raid, Ransome reflected; the kind of raid that could keep an outfit off balance without risk to the attacker.

"Let me go!" Belle insisted, her voice throaty with emotion. And when he turned her loose she ran toward the kitchen stoop where the old cook sprawled unmoving. Risen dust and powder smoke tainted the air; it drifted across the doorway shaft of lamplight in raveled banners.

Big Bart Gillum called, "Git some bandages, Belle — Kid Beauford is hurt!"

Ransome felt around for the saddle and found it. This, he decided, wouldn't be a pleasant place to spend the night. A man might better camp by himself out in the brush. Quickly tightening the cinch he led his horse around behind the barn and rode off at a walk, hoping they wouldn't hear him.

They didn't. . . .

Afterward, crossing the flats east of Circle G, Ransome remembered the fine fragrance of Belle's hair as he'd pressed close to her in the shed. It did things to a man, that fragrance. It made him remember pleasures long discarded. Then the thought came to him that he was riding a dead man's saddle and that realization stirred a dismal sense of foreboding.

CHAPTER 2

Part of the Pattern

Sheriff Sid Baffert was smoking his after-breakfast cigar on the Union Hotel veranda when Doc Smelker drove into Tonto Bend from the west. This was shortly after sunup with dawn's coolness and quiet clinging to the town; with freshly kindled fires sending blue spirals of smoke from chimneys along Residential Avenue while an aged swamper swept discarded cigar butts across the Grand Central Saloon's front stoop.

Baffert, who'd served six consecutive terms as sheriff, watched Smelker leave his rig at Grogan's Livery, not shifting his big-paunched frame from its comfortable sprawl until the young medico came abreast of the veranda. Then Baffert leaned forward and asked, "How's things at Circle G, Doc?"

"The cook died, and Kid Beauford has a broken right arm," John Smelker said wearily. He had brought his new medical kit and his new bride to Tonto Bend five months ago, fresh from an eastern college town. Now he expressed his disapproval of Concho Basin by saying, "That makes five gunshot cases in two weeks' time. I never saw such a lawless country."

"Not a question of law," Baffert offered in a mildly defensive voice. "A sheriff has no jurisdiction in a range war, Doc. He can try to head one off, but he's got no call to interfere after it gets going. That's a job for Rynning's rangers."

"Have you sent for them?" Smelker asked.

Baffert nodded. "They should be showin' up any time."

Smelker sighed and went on, his frowning, scholarly face showing the fatigue of a sleepless night. Watching him turn into Residential Avenue, Sheriff Baffert guessed that the medico couldn't understand why a peace officer should sit idle while men shot at each other in the hills. There'd probably never been a range war where Smelker came from, and there'd been no mention of cow country feuds in the books he'd studied at college. But the rest of Tonto Bend's citizens understood how it was, and why a sheriff couldn't interfere.

Cameo Kimble, who'd spent the night

playing stud poker at the Grand Central, came across Main Street now. His tall, lean-shanked shape cast a long shadow in the early sunlight and Sid Baffert thought: *His shadow might reach all across the Basin one of these days.*

He was an odd one, this Kimble. It occurred to Baffert that no one seemed to know where Cameo came from, nor why he'd chosen to settle in Concho Basin. The sheriff had his own hunch about Cameo, but it didn't quite add up. . . .

Kimble came to the veranda, his milk-blue eyes a trifle bloodshot from watching cards all night, and a black stubble of beard showing on his usually clean shaven face. He had once been a professional gambler and showed it in the manner of his dress. His soiled white shirt, tailored broadcloth coat and striped California pants gave him the appearance of a card-sharp rather than a cowman. A cameo pin adorned his black silk cravat and matching cameo rings decorated the little fingers of both hands. He greeted Baffert with a brash disregard for the old lawman's lack of friendliness, saying, "Fine morning, Sid?"

"Game breakin' up?" Baffert inquired, not much interested.

"No, but I've won my bundle," Kimble said in his bragging, self-satisfied voice. "Now the losers can fight it out among themselves."

He leaned against a veranda post and shaped a cigarette. "Queer thing about losers, Sid. You ever notice how they act in a poker game? They try like hell to beat the winner. They sympathize with each other and gang up on the high stack man, resenting his luck and wanting to chop him down. But when he takes his winnings off the table they turn on each other and to hell with sympathy."

"Yeah," Baffert mused. "That's the way it usually winds up. Every man for himself and the devil take the hindermost."

"Same way in life," Kimble said. "Just another game of grab with a different set of rules. But it adds up to the same thing, which is to git while the gitting's good."

He went on into the dining room then and Baffert heard him greet the waitress with an intimacy that should have made her blush. He thought: *She should hit him over the head with a tray.* But women seldom resented Cameo's romantic boldness. They seemed to like it; seemed to be flattered by it. Even Fay Kane, who'd run a dancehall long enough to recognize a chaser when she saw one, had fallen for Cameo Kimble. According to town gossip she had staked him to a start in the cow business a year ago. Now Kimble's ranch was called Gunman's Camp because of the renegades it harbored and Cameo could call the turn in the Gillum-Tarborrow fight by swinging his hardcase crew to the side he chose. Kimble had stayed out of it, so far; but Sid Baffert had made his sly guess long ago and believed he knew the reason. Cameo wasn't much more than a two-bit cowman, but he had ambitions. And one of them — perhaps the most impelling — didn't concern the acquisition of additional range.

Thinking about that now, Baffert mused, "Cameo has an eye for sweet stuff and there's nothin' sweeter than Belle Gillum."

He sighed, thinking how wrong a match that would be, and how much hell it could cause. Belle Gillum had been courted by every young man in Concho Basin, at one time or another. She'd had her pick of the whole caboodle. . . .

Baffert noticed a rider drop down the stageroad dugway just west of town. Discarding his smoked out cigar, the sheriff watched this newcomer ride in to Grogan's Livery and dismount. A stranger, he decided, and giving the man a contemplative regard, said thoughtfully, "A trifle on the tough side."

Remembering the countless times he'd seen drifters ride into Tonto Bend, Baffert placed his swift and practiced judgment on this one. He tallied the halfbreed holster, thonged at just the correct angle for fast drawing; the bachelor-patched shirt and brush-scuffed boots. As the stranger came along the plank walk Baffert reckoned the black whiskers as being about three days' growth.

As if quoting a reward poster, the sheriff catalogued the details of what he observed: *Six feet tall, weight about one sixty, gray eyes, black hair, age thirty-five, no visible scars.*

There was, he thought, something remotely familiar about the man. But his description didn't fit any of the reward notices; at least not the recent ones. . . .

Lee Ransome, sauntering leisurely along the sidewalk, was also making a mental tally of his observations. The weather-warped false fronts of this town were no different from those in Texas Junction, Willcox, or a dozen other cowtowns he'd known. The same gnawed hitchracks and horse droppings in front of mercantile establishments, saloon and hotel; even the rubbish-littered vacant lot at the corner of Ringo Alley looked familiar, and so did the two-story Dixie Dancehall that rose beyond it. The illusion of sameness was complete when he noticed that the dancehall sign contained the inscription: *"Fay Kane, prop."* Five years ago she'd been a sweet-voiced singer in the Bon Ton at Texas Junction.

Ransome frowned, all the bitter, corroding memories crowding in on him again. The past, he thought morosely, was never far behind a man; regardless of how long a trail he rode the past was no farther than the sight of a familiar face, or a name, or the mind-mirrored vision of a girl bleeding to death on a hotel veranda.

Continuing his slow march along the deserted sidewalk, Ransome peered at the county courthouse with its steepled belfry which stood at the intersection of Main Street and Residential Avenue. If Jim Tarborrow had told the truth there stood a monument to the injustice this town had done him. The verdict twelve men had reached in there might have been a variety-show mockery of justice — a cheap travesty that had doomed an innocent man to exile in Yuma Prison. And they had unwittingly doomed Concho Basin to the ruin of range war.

Ransome was within a dozen yards of the hotel steps when he identified Sheriff Baffert by the sun-glinted star on his vest. It was characteristic of Lee Ransome that he made no effort to avoid a face-to-face meeting. There'd been many times in the past when he could have side-stepped trouble by merely crossing a street or turning his back on a town where the game was rigged against him. But at such times he invariably remembered the counsel of his Confederate cavalryman father: "You can't side-step your share of trouble, son. Nor run away from it. You might as well hit it head-on."

And so it was now. Baffert, he supposed, had been watching him since the moment he rode into town. It would be simple, of course, to explain his presence here. But Captain Rynning had advised against it. The Ranger boss wasn't sure about the sheriff, he surmised that Baffert was just a badge-toting politician astraddle of a fence; but the sheriff might even have helped frame Jim Tarborrow. In which case it would be better to work alone on the case. . . .

Ransome mounted the hotel veranda,

ignoring Baffert's presence until the sheriff rose from his chair and asked, "Figgerin' to spend some time in town, stranger?"

"Yeah," Ransome said, and met the lawman's sharp-eyed appraisal with an indifference that bordered on brashness. "Any objections?"

Baffert didn't like that, and showed it in the way his faded eyes took flame. "Maybe yes, maybe no," he announced. "What's your business here?"

"Personal," Ransome said flatly.

"That's no answer at all," Baffert objected. He tapped the star on his vest with a big-knuckled finger, saying, "It's my job to question suspicious strangers."

"Do I look suspicious?" Ransome inquired.

Baffert glanced deliberately at the tied-down gungear and nodded and demanded, "What's your business here?"

"Breakfast, for one thing," Ransome said, matching the lawman's gruff tone.

"Maybe you'll eat it in jail," Baffert suggested. "Maybe you'll be more civil in a cell."

He was, Ransome realized, a thoroughly game old rooster. There'd been a deceptive mildness in his voice at first; he had looked like just another well-fed politician wearing a badge. But that, Ransome decided now, was a mistaken impression. There was courage behind the badge, and a stubborn pride in wearing it.

Baffert's right hand was close to holster. He asked harshly, "You talkin' — or goin' to jail?"

"Don't try it," Ransome warned. "Don't try to jail me now or any time."

He was aware of someone standing in the lobby doorway, but his attention was focused strictly on this star-packer who stood teetering on the thin edge of grabbing his gun. And because a show-down now might lessen his chance of finding the man he sought, Ransome said, "When I finish eating breakfast I'm heading for Cameo Kimble's place."

It was a concession to Baffert's demand. It allowed the sheriff to refrain from further action without losing face. Yet now an increased sharpness came into his questing eyes and he exclaimed, "I thought you reminded me of somebody. Now, by God, I know who!"

That puzzled Ransome completely. Why should mention of Kimble cause Baffert to recognize him? What possible connection could there be? Hell, he'd never met the man.

Baffert answered those questions by saying, "You look enough like Kimble to be his brother. Are you?"

Which was when Cameo Kimble eased out of the doorway, saying, "No, just a cousin," and offering his hand to Ransome, said smilingly, "Long time no see."

"Yeah," Ransome agreed, attempting to conceal his surprise. "A long time, for a fact."

Then he asked, "Are they still serving breakfast in there, Cameo? I'm hungry as six Sonora steers."

"Sure," Kimble said, ushering Ransome toward the lobby doorway. "Best food west of the Pecos."

Sheriff Baffert watched them go into the hotel dining room. "Another tough one," he muttered soberly and, remembering the devil-be-damned brashness he'd seen in the stranger's eyes, added, "Tougher than Cameo."

He glanced at the clock in the court-house belfry, and seeing that the time was twenty minutes past nine, went slowly across Main Street. There was a set pattern to this sauntering, roundabout trip he took three or four times a week. He looked in at the Grand Central poker game, observing by the arrangement of chips how the luck was going, then strolled to the livery stable for a brief visit with his good friend Grogan. Recalling that the stranger had left his horse here, he asked, "What's the brand on the roan that just came in, Pat?"

"Looks like a Roman Four, near as I can call it," Grogan said. A sly twinkle came into his eyes and he asked, "You got him figgered out, Sid — the tall one with the tied-down holster?"

"He's some kin to Cameo Kimble," Baffert said. "It don't take much figgerin' to tell what he is."

Grogan nodded agreement. "He's got a spalpeen look in his eye, bejasus — a rank, go-to-hell look."

Baffert walked on, and turning into Ringo Alley, took the outside stairway that led to Fay Kane's living quarters above the Dixie Dancehall. It was nine forty now, and Fay invariably put the coffeepot on at nine thirty. She heard him coming up the stairs, and had the door open for him.

"Just in time for coffee," she greeted, which was also a part of the pattern along with the red silk kimono she wore, and her sleep-swollen eyes. "Anything new or exciting in town this morning?"

"Not much. A cousin of Kimble's rode

in from the west and is eatin' breakfast with Cameo at the hotel."

That seemed to surprise her for she asked, "When did Cameo ride in?"

"Yesterday evenin'," Baffert reported and watched her pour the coffee. When she sat down at the table he said, "You'd best forget him, Fay. He's a counterfeit if ever I saw one."

It was in his mind to tell her that Kimble wanted a younger woman; that the boss of Gunman's Camp had honeyfussed her for the sole purpose of borrowing money. But the haunted expression in her eyes kept him from saying it. Instead he reached over and patted her arm and said, "I been waitin' a long time, Fay. I'll keep on waitin'."

And when she smiled at him, Baffert thought: *She looks good to me, even in the morning.*

CHAPTER 3

"Look Out!"

When the waitress had taken his order, Lee Ransome gave Kimble a frankly appraising contemplation. "So you're the big gun Fred Lomax told me about," he said.

A sardonic amusement showed in Cameo's pale blue eyes and rutted his high-boned face. Except for the sensual, almost feminine fullness of his lips, he had the look of a man who'd take a lot of licking.

"What did Lomax tell you about me?" Kimble inquired.

"He said you were running a gunman's camp, and might take over the whole caboodle in time," Ransome reported, quoting Jim Tarborrow's guess as to Kimble's strategy.

Cameo's chuckle seemed a trifle forced. "Where would Lomax get a notion like that?" he scoffed. "Fred must of gone a trifle loco in jail — stir crazy they call it."

But he didn't deny the possibility; instead he added sharply, "Don't go spreading that opinion around."

"Sounds like an order," Ransome suggested, not liking the arrogant tone of it.

Kimble's eyes narrowed and his lips took on the pursed pout of a man about to whistle. "Maybe you heard it right," he said.

Ransome shrugged, said casually, "I'm not in the habit of taking orders until I'm on a payroll."

"Well, ain't you signing on with me?" Kimble asked. "Ain't that why you was headed to my place?"

"Sort of," Ransome admitted. "But I was figuring to look your outfit over first."

No use to appear overly anxious, he thought. Kimble wouldn't be an easy man to fool; he had a sharp look to him.

The waitress brought his breakfast. She smiled at Kimble, who helped her arrange the dishes with an exaggerated gallantry. *He's got a romeo streak in him,* Ransome reflected, tallying this impression and weighing it against what Jim Tarborrow had told him. Cameo, he decided, had some surprisingly contrasting characteristics for a Wild Bunch boss. The man seemed capable of shifting personality with the professional ease of a variety stage actor. . . .

When the waitress left the table, Ransome asked, "How come you called me your cousin?"

"Just a little joke on Sid, who prides himself at remembering faces," Kimble explained. Then his eyes narrowed and he asked, "How do I know for sure that Fred Lomax sent you?"

Ransome dug out the note and handed it over. "That should explain things all around," he muttered and went at his food with a hungry man's eagerness. There was a bare possibility that Cameo was familiar with Lomax's handwriting; but the risk seemed remote, for the rustler hadn't looked like a man who'd write letters.

"Lee Ransome," Kimble mused thoughtfully. He peered up at the ceiling in the squinting, intent fashion of a man searching his memory. "Weren't you town marshal of a couple towns in Texas a few years ago — the one they called the Killer Kid Marshal?"

Ransome nodded, understanding that this was the acid test of the scheme Tom Rynning had concocted. If he could make this sound reasonable or plausible there'd be no trouble getting into Gunman's

Camp. "I got the town taming idea after my sister was killed by a stray bullet in Texas Junction," he explained. "But it was a sorry way to make a living."

"So you tried an easier way and got sent to Yuma for getting caught," Kimble chuckled. Then he asked, "Did you run into Jim Tarborrow at Yuma?"

"Had the next cell to him," Ransome announced. "He got railroaded, same as me, which is one reason I came here for a looksee."

Kimble laughed. He said scoffingly, "I'd bet my boots against a plugged peso that every man in Yuma claims he was railroaded. You don't really think Tarborrow was innocent, do you?"

Ransome nodded and, deciding on a bold play, said flatly, "I aim to find the dirty son who framed him."

That seemed to tickle Cameo. He asked laughingly, "Would you recognize him if you saw him?"

"I think so," Ransome said, not quite sure about this. "There was one odd thing about him that I'd notice."

Curiosity was plain in Cameo's eyes when he asked, "Is the clue a secret?"

Ransome nodded and went on with his eating. A man had to watch his step in a game like this; had to watch his tongue also. Seeming to give his whole attention to the food before him, he covertly watched Kimble and soon discovered that Cameo was as covertly watching him.

He's not entirely convinced, Ransome thought; in fact he sensed outright suspicion in Kimble. Wondering as to the reason, he tried to guess which part of his brief recitation had sounded false, and couldn't identify it. Perhaps the brevity of his talk was the flaw; a man who'd been in jail would be apt to ask many questions.

So thinking, Ransome asked, "What side of the Gillum-Tarborrow fracas are you on?"

"Didn't Jim Tarborrow tell you?" Kimble asked.

Ransome recognized the trick in that question. He said, "Jim seemed to think you were straddling the fence, last he heard."

"That's right," Kimble said. "I'm on neither side, so far."

And then he winked slyly in the way of a secretive man giving an implication of possessing important information which wasn't to be divulged. There was, Ransome decided, a smart-alecky streak in Cameo. He had the flash vanity of a gambler accustomed to winning; a gambler who might be a very poor loser.

"I'm smackdab in the middle," Kimble explained, "which would be a bad position, except that I've got some real salty boys riding for me."

"So I've heard," Ransome said, and was abruptly eager to investigate the crew at Gunman's Camp. With a little luck this deal might be soon over. "Lomax," he suggested, "said you paid gun wages."

"Top pay for top men," Kimble acknowledged. "Want to go look the outfit over?" Ransome nodded, whereupon Kimble bragged, "You'll never see a tougher bunch than I've collected. By God they're beauts."

Afterward, as they rode out of town, he warned, "Better not let on you're looking for anybody, friend Lee. Those boys might take you for a law spy."

Then he turned to face Ransome directly, saying, "So that's why you want to give my place a looksee. You've got a hunch the man that framed Tarborrow might be riding for me."

Ransome nodded, and wondered why that admission seemed to amuse Kimble. Cameo understood now that one of his crew might be the target he sought, yet that knowledge didn't disturb Kimble at all. Instead he took it as a joke. The man must have a sadistic sense of humor, Ransome decided.

Presently, as they climbed into timber, Ransome said, "I'll make a deal, Cameo. You forget I'm a friend of Jim Tarborrow and I'll forget what Lomax told me about you taking over Concho Basin."

"That's a bargain," Kimble agreed smilingly. He shaped up a cigarette with agile fingers that were unmarked by rope burn or callus. They were the hands of a gambler, Ransome reflected, and noticed for the first time that a ring adorned each of the little fingers.

Observing his interest Kimble said, "Won 'em in my first big poker game. They brought me luck, and I never took them off since."

Then, as a rider galloped around a bend in the stageroad, he said sharply, "Here comes trouble!"

Ransome watched the rider pull his sweat-lathered horse to a halt, heard Kimble inquire, "What's the rush, Tate?" and guessed at once that the newcomer was Tate Tarborrow, boss of Bootjack. Temper burned in the man's jet-black eyes and a scowl rutted his dark, high-beaked face as he demanded, "Is Doc Smelker in town?"

"Yes," Kimble said. "What's the trouble?"

"Gillums raided our roundup camp," Tarborrow announced angrily. "Dirty sons caught us in our bedrolls. Sam got a slug in the chest and looks like a goner."

He glanced at Kimble's horse, said, "I could use a fresh pony."

"Sure," Kimble agreed.

While they were stripping saddles and transferring them, Tarborrow asked, "Who's your friend?"

"My cousin Lee," Kimble said, winking at Ransome.

"Lee who?" Tarborrow demanded.

Seizing this opportunity to forestall a need for seeming friendliness with the Tarborrows, Ransome announced, "Just Lee. Doesn't that suit you?"

Tarborrow reared back as though he'd been slapped. "Don't you sass me!" he shouted. "When I ask straight questions I want straight answers, by God!"

"You're wasting time," Kimble counseled. "Ten minutes might mean the difference between living and dying for your brother Sam."

"It sure might," Tarborrow muttered. He wiped his perspiring face on a greasy sleeve of his buckskin jacket and climbed hastily into saddle. "I'll drop by your place and pick up my horse," he said, then jabbed his fresh mount with blood-stained spurs.

"Red rowel Tate," Kimble mused, watching Tarborrow gallop off at a dead run. He nodded at the raw gouges on the panting Bootjack pony and added, "Tate rides like he fights — for blood. Reckon it's that quarter strain of Injun that the Tarborrows got in their veins."

Then he asked, "Say, you know who that was?"

"A Tarborrow?" Ransome asked.

"Jim Tarborrow's father," Kimble chuckled, "and you made him mad enough to grab a gun."

"He's nothing to me," Ransome muttered, wanting to seem resentful. "I don't like nosey galoots asking my last name like it was their right to know."

Presently, as they continued on up the stageroad, he said, "It didn't take Gillum long to pay back the raid."

"Who told you about Circle G being raided?" Kimble asked, plainly surprised that Ransome should know about it.

"Happened while I was there," Ransome reported.

"You was at Circle G?"

Ransome told him about the mishap on Mormon Ridge, and Belle Gillum's kindness in replacing the smashed saddle. "She's real nice," he concluded, "even if her name is Gillum."

"What the hell has her name got to do with it?" Kimble demanded. "Don't go taking for gospel truth all that stuff Jim Tarborrow told you about the Gillums."

A brightness warmed Kimble's pale eyes and he added gustily, "There ain't another goddam woman in Arizona Territory can compare with Belle Gillum. Not one!"

That passionate declaration surprised Ransome and puzzled him. Cameo must be whole-hog high on Big Bart's daughter. If he felt that way about Belle why wasn't he siding her father? And why was he on friendly terms with Tate Tarborrow?

As if guessing those questions, Cameo said, "She's a trifle choosy, which is her right. But she'll change when the time comes."

"What time?" Ransome prompted.

A confident smile loosened Kimble's moist, full lips. "When Circle G has to have my help or go under," he announced, seeming quite sure about this. "When a man with some salty gunhawks on his payroll would make Big Bart a real handy son-in-law."

So that was the reason Cameo Kimble played a waiting game — a romantic reason that Jim Tarborrow hadn't known about. It seemed odd that a man's romantic notions should play so important a part in the blood-spattered destiny of Concho Basin. And equally odd that a Wild Bunch boss of Kimble's caliber should be so smitten by a woman's charms. Judging by the way Cameo had flirted with the hotel waitress, Ransome guessed that he'd had his share of women. More than his share, most likely. Kimble, he supposed, had a campfire vision in his head — a wondrous, flame-fashioned image of the woman all men dreamed of and few ever found.

Ransome smiled cynically, remembering that he'd once had the same dream. There'd been a homestead in his dream, for the woman to share — all the pleasant trimmings that went with a wife. But that was before he had watched his sister Nancy bleed to death one tragic day in Texas Junction; before he'd stood at her grave with the salty bite of tears in his eyes and dedicated his gun to a vengeance crusade against careless killers.

Again, as it had so many times, the scene came back to him. He'd stood on the Alamo Hotel veranda with Nancy, admiring the new hat she had just purchased at the millinery shop. He had told her how elegant she looked. "Prettiest girl in all Texas," he'd bragged and she had said, "Oh, Lee!"

Which was when two drunken renegades opened fire on each other out in the street. A half dozen shots in swift succession, and one of those bullets struck Nancy with a sickening impact. She had loosed a frantic scream as she slumped against him. Blood had bubbled from her girlish breast as he eased her gently down to the veranda's dusty boards. She had sobbed like a little girl afraid to be alone in the dark. She'd said again, "Oh, Lee!" and died in his arms.

Ransome grimaced, remembering each detail. He had faced the street and damned the man who stood with a smoking gun in his hand. He had slammed three bullets into that man and cursed him as he fell, then emptied his gun at the other renegade's sprawled shape. But even that hadn't been enough to kill the awful need for vengeance and so he had become a killer lawman at the age of twenty-three.

That, too, had been futile. Instead of helping him forget, it had seemed to keep the wound of grief from healing; to keep it raw year after smoky year while men called him a cold-blooded merciless machine of legal execution. Until the hate had finally burned out of him and he could smile again — could even make plans for the homestead he'd always wanted. So he had come to Arizona, wanting to make a fresh, clean start, and met his old friend Tom Rynning who'd become captain of the Rangers.

The favor Rynning had asked didn't make sense to Lee Ransome at first. "If it's a gunhawk you need why don't you use Jeff Kidder, or Billy Olds, or Timberline Sparks?" he'd demanded, knowing the reputation those men had made themselves.

But Rynning had shook his head. "They're all known Rangers," he explained. "They'd be spotted the minute they stepped foot in Tonto Bend and have both factions gunning for them. A range feud is a touchy thing, Lee. I don't want my outfit implicated directly if it can be avoided."

And now he was riding toward Gunman's Camp with a man who made a business of collecting renegades. . . .

Leaving the stageroad, Kimble angled into a trail that led up the steep side of Rimrock Reef, a long jagged upthrust that reared high above the surrounding country. "Short cut," he explained and urged the fagged Bootjack pony up a series of tortuous switch-backs.

It was long past noon, with sun's heat radiating from slab rock formations, when they halted on the summit. Perspiration beaded Kimble's forehead beneath his nudged-back hat. He dug out a bandana and wiped his face in the fastidious fashion of an aristocratic gentleman. Then he pointed to a tree-bordered clearing directly below the ridge and announced, "My headquarters."

Not much to look at, Ransome reflected. Two log cabins, one of them long and obviously a bunkhouse; a wagon shed, corrals and windmill. Except for the extra cabin it might have been the sorry abode of a poverty-stricken homesteader.

"I control the range you see between here and Concho Rim, except for Luke Beauford's ranch in Homestead Valley," Kimble bragged. "I took over places on each side of him a month ago — family men that got scared out on account of the Gillum-Tarborrow feud. They saw what was coming and didn't like the smell of it."

Kimble chuckled, adding, "I use their places for line camps with two men in each one. Beauford says he won't sell, but he might change his mind later on."

"Is Beauford siding with the Gillums?" Ransome asked, thinking about the Kid Beauford he'd met at Circle G.

"No, nor he ain't with the Tarborrows either," Cameo said. "Which seems downright comical, considering that his boy left home and Beauford ain't much of a hand with a gun. You've got to take one side or the other in this country, or have a crew like mine."

It was, Ransome guessed, a casual way of saying that Cameo intended to crowd Luke Beauford off his place when he got around to it. The boss of Gunman's Camp could play a waiting game, reasonably certain that the bloody feud between Bootjack and Circle G would favor his range-grabbing plans.

"Yonder, to the west is Gillum's outfit," Cameo directed. Then he faced east, saying, "You can't see Tarborrow's ranch, but it lies just beyond the saddle in that piney divide. Lots of good graze all over this end of the Basin."

"So I've noticed," Ransome said with a

cowman's eye for grass and water and browse. It would make a rich cattle kingdom for a thoroughly greedy man, if he was strong enough to grab it. . . .

They had slid their horses down a final chute-like drop from Rimrock Reef and were crossing a timbered slope when a gnome-faced dwarfish man on a grulla mare emerged from behind a windfall.

"Hi, Frenchy," Kimble greeted.

A happy smile creased the rider's wizened face. He uttered an inarticulate, gurgling bleat that was half wail, half chuckle, and gazed at Kimble with dog-like devotion as Cameo said, "This is Frenchy Meusette, best cook and camp guard in Arizona Territory."

Meusette's brown eyes shone with pleasure. They were, Ransome thought, like the meek liquid eyes of a tail-wagging dog wanting affection. Meusette cupped a childishly small hand and raised it to his lips as if drinking, then whirled the mare and rode off at a lope.

Kimble chuckled. "There'll be hot coffee waiting for us," he predicted. "The Apaches caught Frenchy over in the Whetstones. They'd scalped him and cut off his tongue when I found him. He rates me one notch higher than God. Hates to have me out of his sight."

"Reminds me of an airedale I owned in Texas," Ransome said. "Same look in his eyes, and the same sounding bark of welcome when I came home."

"I don't suppose he's the payroll bandit you're looking for," Kimble suggested with sly derision.

Ransome shook his head and presently, as they rode into the ranch yard, he saw a tall man dousing his face at the wash bench outside the bunkhouse doorway. A pair of riding gloves, protruding from a hip pocket, caught Ransome's attention at once and he thought with swift rising anticipation: *That might be the bandit!*

"Who's the jigger washing up?" he asked, forcing a casual tone.

"Society Slim, who got drummed out of the cavalry for shooting a brother officer in a fight over a swivel-rumped woman," Kimble said. While they unsaddled at the corral he added, "Slim ain't set foot in a town within fifty miles of an Army post since."

"Has he been around this country long?" Ransome inquired.

"Couple years, I guess. He got run off Hashknife for pulling a gun on the range foreman in a poker game. He talks real

57

fancy, and takes a bath oftener than most folks, but don't get the idea he's a gentle Annie when it comes to fighting. He's a ring-tailed heller from here to who hid the broom."

Two men were holding down a rope-trussed bronc while a third fitted a shoe to a hind foot. All three of them stared at Ransome now, and the man with the horseshoe — a barrel-shaped tough with red hair and a beefy, brutal face — demanded in an astonishingly high-pitched voice, "Who are you?"

Ransome grinned, amused that so pugnacious a man should have such a falsetto tone. But he ignored the redhead, giving Society Slim a calculating appraisal. According to Jim Tarborrow the masked bandit who held him up had been a tallish man, and although it had been a warm summer day *he had worn a pair of gloves.*

"Look out!" Kimble warned.

CHAPTER 4

Simple Slaughter

Lee Ransome dodged, but something glanced along his left temple with a searing burn. His left hand rose instinctively to touch the raw flesh. He examined the blood on his fingers, not quite sure what had hit him. Then he saw the horseshoe in the dust, and heard the redhead exclaim, "That'll learn you not to laugh at me, by God!"

They were all watching him now, Ransome realized. They were wondering what he would do. . . .

"Red is a trifle touchy," Kimble said, the amusement in his eyes making a mockery of his sympathetic tone. He was, Ransome guessed, secretly pleased at Red's demonstration of toughness. It backed Cameo's brag about his salty crew. As if giving formal introductions at a social function, Kimble announced, "Meet the boys you'll be riding with, friend Lee. Red Surdine is my foreman. The two gentlemen behind him are Hack Benson and Joe Tanner. Men, this is Lee Ransome."

Surdine peered questioningly at Ransome, keeping his right hand close to holster. He asked gruffly, "Ain't you the one that made a big rep in Texas four five years ago?"

"Yeah," Ransome muttered. The shock of the blow faded from his temple, swift anger replacing it. But there was no sign of resentment on his face as he stepped forward, saying in friendly fashion, "Glad to meet you, Red."

Bug-eyed with astonishment, Surdine reached for the hand Ransome offered. He was like that, completely confused and wide open, when Ransome hit him in the belly.

Red loosed a shrill curse and narrowly dodged the left Ransome swung at his face. "Why you dirty stinkin' bastard!" Surdine shrilled. Then he lunged in, swinging both fists.

Ransome smiled thinly, guessing at once that Red's temper had the best of him. There was such a thing as blind rage and this man was like a bull charging with his eyes closed. Deftly side-stepping Surdine's rush, Ransome connected with a vicious left hook that sliced a raw furrow of flesh from Surdine's jaw, then whirling in behind him, hammered Red above the kidneys with both fists.

Surdine wheeled in time to hit Ransome in the chest, a solid smash that knocked the wind out of him. That single blow warned Ransome of the terrific power behind Red's massive arms, and he thought: *I'll have to outguess him.* Momentarily blocking the redhead's clubbing fists, Ransome retreated, and sucked great gulps of air into his aching lungs.

"I'll learn you!" Surdine blurted, a wild eagerness in his hot eyes. "By God I'll learn you good!"

Wholly on the defensive now, Ransome backed slowly, moving in a circle while risen dust made a sun-sparkled fog, and Hack Benson urged gleefully, "Dab it on him, Red — dab it on!"

Society Slim sauntered over from the bunkhouse and asked casually, "Who's our fisticuffing guest?"

"Drifter named Ransome," Kimble muttered, absorbed in what seemed to be the final moments of this fight.

Ransome took a glancing blow on the right shoulder, turning with it and drawing Red off balance. He swung at Red's face, and missed and took a jolting blow to the ribs. That one hurt; it spun him half way around and brought a hoot of derisive laughter from Hack Benson. But Ransome remained on his feet and craftily side-stepped Surdine's continuing attack. He had his wind back now, and a sure knowl-edge of what would happen if this redhead succeeded in knocking him down. A gloating, merciless brutality shone in Red's bull-like eyes and a drooling lust was on his loose-lipped mouth. He would boot a man's ribs in, Ransome thought, and laugh while doing it.

Crouching and weaving; shifting warily from Surdine's head-on charges, Ransome fought with an angerless calculating skill. He hit Red with a darting uppercut to the midriff, took two wildly swung blows on his blocking arms, then targeted Red's bul-bous nose with a sledging punch that knocked the burly one back on his heels.

When Ransome rushed in, Joe Tanner yelled, "Boot him, Red — crotch him!"

Surdine attempted to follow that advice. But Ransome grabbed his upthrust boot, wrenching it sideways and spilling Red to his knees. With the frantic, tooth-bared snarl of a cornered coyote, Surdine snatched his gun from holster. He fired once, that bullet slanting past Ransome as his boot kicked the gun from Surdine's grasp. Ransome hit him in the nose again while Red scrambled to his feet; he was remotely aware of a commotion at the hitchrack, and glimpsed Frenchy Meusette rushing across the yard.

Blood spurted from Surdine's flaring nostrils. He staggered sideways, and covered his face as if fearing further punishment of his battered nose. Ransome slugged him in the belly in the deliberate fashion of a man knowing exactly what was needed, and doing it. As Surdine lowered his guard to protect his midriff Ransome slammed rights and lefts into Red's pulpy face with the cool precision of a butcher slicing meat.

Blinded by blood and squawling high-pitched curses, Surdine endeavored to dodge away. He tripped and was going down when Ransome clutched him by the shirtfront and propped him up with the seeming gentleness of a man aiding a drunken companion. Ransome had uttered no word, and didn't now, but a wicked exultation glinted his smoky eyes as he hit Surdine under the left ear with a chopping right.

Surdine's head wabbled. His knees buckled so that only Ransome's continuing support held him upright. He stared dully as Ransome measured him for a final blow, offering no resistance. But instead of hitting him, Ransome said flatly, "Go pick up the horseshoe, Red."

Surdine's bruised lips loosed a shuddering sigh. He wiped his bleeding nose on an upraised arm and asked thickly, "What for?"

"Because I said so," Ransome ordered, cuffing him with an open palm. "Go pick it up."

Surdine gawked at him in bafflement. There was no animosity in Ransome's voice — none of the bully brashness of victory. But Red recognized the rank toughness he saw in Ransome's eyes. Moving with the uncertainty of a man close to drunkenness, he stepped over to the horseshoe and picked it up.

Ransome drew his gun and fired without seeming to take aim. The explosion and Surdine's yelp were simultaneous. The bullet had knocked the horseshoe from Red's grasp, the impact stinging his fingers so that he shook them like a man who'd picked up a hot branding iron.

"Just wanted you to know how it feels to get burned by a cold horseshoe," Ransome explained and holstered his gun.

For a moment no one moved or spoke. And in this hushed interval Frenchy Meusette's inarticulate whimpering attracted Ransome's attention to the hitchrack where the little cook crouched beside the fallen grulla mare. Red's bullet, Ransome guessed, had killed Frenchy's horse.

But Cameo Kimble and his crew weren't watching Meusette. They were peering at the man whose bruised knuckles had pounded Red Surdine into submission; whose gunskill had knocked a horseshoe from the foreman's fingers with such flashing accuracy. It was an old and familiar scene to Lee Ransome. He had witnessed this same center of calculating attention a hundred times in Texas, and understood it thoroughly. Except for Surdine, whose gun lay in the dust, these men were wondering if they could match his draw. Wondering, and itching to find out. Prodded by personal vanity one of them would seek the answer any moment now. The pattern never changed. Only the names and faces were different. . . .

Joe Tanner's pock-pitted face took on a tighter and tighter appearance; all his features seeming to be drawn inward by the force of his thinking. *Cocking himself*, Ransome recognized; mentally thumbing his courage, like a man cocking a gun.

Hack Benson, who resembled Surdine for beefiness, kept wetting his lower lip with the tip of his tongue, like a man anticipating a tasty dish and barely able to resist reaching for it.

Society Slim and Cameo Kimble stood motionless; rigidly attentive. Only Surdine, who wiped his perspiring, blood-smeared face, seemed relaxed.

Ransome kept his right hand close to holster, and waited, and was aware of an increasing soreness in the knuckles of that poised hand. A gunhawk, he reflected, was a fool to fight with his fists. A crippled right hand could cost him his life. The momentary fumble of a stiff fingered or swollen hand might mean the difference between living and dying.

Joe Tanner took out his Durham sack, deftly fashioned a cigarette and put it between his lips. Then he glanced at Ransome, asked, "Have a smoke?" and tossed the tobacco sack.

It was an old trick, tarnished by long usage. A tinhorn trick calculated to give a sure-thing advantage to the man who worked it. But Lee Ransome had seen it played three years ago; he said, "Not now," and watched Tanner's right hand, not relaxing until the beefy rider reached into a vest pocket for a match.

"That was nice shooting, hitting the horseshoe," Society Slim said. "Very nice shooting indeed."

That broke the spell. Hack Benson chuckled, saying, "Red sure dropped it tol'able quick. You'd of thought it was on fire."

Cameo Kimble smiled. He peered at Surdine and said, "Lee should make us a good hand, eh Red?"

Surdine was still a trifle groggy, but he had a remnant of pride remaining. "Not while I'm here," he muttered.

Joe Tanner laughed and Society Slim said amusedly, "Red can't abide a man who's able to outpunch him, Mister Ransome. If he had knocked you down Red would want you on the crew. It's the top-sergeant streak in him."

There was no amusement in Kimble's voice when he asked, "What do you mean — while you're here, Red?"

"Just what I said," Surdine muttered stubbornly. "There ain't room enough on this outfit for me and him both."

Kimble asked quietly, "You wouldn't quit me, would you, Red?"

Surdine kept mopping his face. Both

sleeves were bloodstained from wrist to shoulder now, and one eye was swollen shut. "I ain't runnin' no crew with him on it," he insisted. "If he stays, I go."

Watching this, and understanding it was none of his affair, Ransome saw Kimble's lips purse into the same whistling pout he'd observed at the hotel. It was, he guessed, a sure sign of temper in Cameo. And it held some startling significance for Red Surdine who exclaimed abruptly, "All right, Cameo — I'll stay!"

"Sure," Kimble said smoothly. A satisfied smile creased his black-bristled cheeks now and his voice fairly dripped graciousness. "You'll stay, Red, and you'll never tell Sid Baffert what you know. That's for sure."

Then, picking up Surdine's gun, Kimble turned to Frenchy Meusette and said, "Too bad about your mare, Frenchy."

Tears shone in Meusette's eyes as he got up and peered at Cameo, uttering a wailed and wordless babble which Kimble seemed to understand.

"It was Red," Cameo announced.

Then he held out the foreman's gun.

"Don't give him that gun!" Surdine shouted.

He rushed forward as if to intercept the

transfer, then halted with both hands held palm outward toward the little cook. It was, Ransome thought, almost comical; Surdine so big and brutish standing there with fear blanching his battered slack-jawed face — appealing to a dwarfish little man who had tears in his eyes. A ridiculous thing, loco as a drunkard's dream. . . .

Ransome saw Meusette glance questioningly at Kimble, saw Cameo nod, and heard Hack Benson announce with callous indifference, "You're a gone goose, Red."

The last tattered remnant of Surdine's pride dissolved so that fear was a naked shameful thing in his face. A prideless, pleading thing. "No, Frenchy — no!" he screamed, and was running frantically toward the wagon shed when Meusette fired.

It was slaughter. Pure and simple slaughter. The first bullet knocked Surdine off stride so that he swerved drunkenly. He loosed a screeching falsetto wail as the second slug, ripping through his right shoulder, spun him around like a grotesque, wabbling top. Meusette drove three more bullets into the reeling redhead as he slowly collapsed.

Ransome, who'd seen his full share of killings, was sickened by this one. It went against the grain to watch a fist-battered, unarmed man die without a chance. Even so low a man as Surdine. He glanced at Kimble, and saw about what he had expected to see: sardonic amusement.

"Red got too goddam big for his britches," Cameo announced. He watched Frenchy Meusette walk toward the house, then said, "A couple of you boys saddle up and drag that mare off into the brush. Take her far enough so Frenchy won't be smelling the stink. He thought more of that grulla than most men think of their wives."

"What about Red?" Society Slim asked in his crisp, cultured voice.

"Put him in the wagon," Kimble directed. "He'll keep till morning."

Then, as the three riders moved off toward the corral, Kimble looked at Ransome and asked, "You going to ride for me?"

There was nothing in his voice to indicate that the matter was important, one way or the other. But Ransome sensed that it was important and understood that Kimble, being short a man, would resent refusal. In which case Cameo might make it difficult for his invited guest to leave, alive. This wasn't just a warrior outfit. It

70

was a hell camp of loco killers. But the deciding factor was Ransome's wish to watch Society Slim; to discover if the renegade cavalryman was the bandit he sought.

"Well?" Kimble prompted.

"Yes," Ransome said.

Whereupon Kimble smiled, saying, "You'll take Red's place."

"Not as foreman," Ransome objected. "Promote somebody else to that job."

But Kimble shook his head. "You're just the man for the job," he announced.

And something in the way he said it warned Lee Ransome. . . .

CHAPTER 5

A Fatal Flaw

Kid Beauford sat in the Circle G kitchen with his broken right arm supported by a sling and watched Belle Gillum make baking powder biscuits. She looked real nice, standing there at the table with a red-checked apron on her. Nicer, even, than she looked in riding clothes. So gosh darn nice it gave him a funny feeling just to look at her. She was, he guessed, the prettiest woman in Arizona. Or in the whole wide world.

But presently, as Belle glanced at him and said smilingly, "A penny for your thoughts," Kid Beauford couldn't find the right words to tell her how he felt. It was always like this. He could think of fancy speeches when he was off alone, riding in the brush. He could tell his horse exactly what he thought about her and how he felt deep down inside. But he could never come by the right words when she was

72

with him. So now he shrugged and said, "I was just thinkin'."

"About what?" she prompted.

Kid Beauford blushed. If she ever found out some of the things he'd thought; private things, like how it would be to have her for a wife. To see her in a nightgown. . . .

"Well, about you, mostly," he admitted.

Belle quit looking at him then. She sprinkled some flour on the bread dough she was mixing and asked, "Does your arm still ache?"

"Not much," he said. "Not enough to mention."

He watched her flour-dusted fingers skillfully maneuver dough into a large pan. They had a nice shape to them, so slim and long; like her legs when she wore denim riding pants. He blushed again, remembering how the faded denim fitted her in back. She was shaped the way a woman should be; she purely was. . . .

"It must have hurt awful when the bullet hit you," Belle suggested.

"Yes ma'am, but not nearly as bad as I'd figgered it would. Always thought gittin' shot would be a hundred times worse than havin' a tooth pulled. But it wasn't that bad."

"It was, for poor Cookie," Belle said and glanced out the window at the ranch graveyard on a flat-topped knoll nearby. "At this time yesterday Cookie was making the biscuits for supper," she mused soberly. "Now he's up there with Uncle Clem and Uncle Harley."

Belle sighed, and stood for a moment peering at the wooden crosses above rock-piled mounds. She said bleakly, "I wonder who'll be next."

"Hard tellin'," Kid Beauford said. "The way things happen it might be most anybody at all. Puts me in mind of what my daddy said when the trouble first started. It didn't seem sensible to me then. It sounded like a lot of jawbone jabber. But I guess it wasn't."

"What did he say?" Belle inquired.

"There was quite a lot to it which I disremember, but the main part was that no matter who won a range war, everybody lost."

Belle nodded agreement. "Your father is right, Kid. But sometimes being right isn't enough."

"Such as?"

"Well, sometimes you have to use guns, regardless," Belle explained. "Everyone knows Big Bart didn't want to use guns against the Tarborrows. But he had no choice."

The Kid wasn't much interested in that. He said, "You sure look real nice in an apron, ma'am, and with your sleeves rolled up. I guess nobody ever looked nicer."

"Why thank you, sir," Belle exclaimed smilingly.

"I ain't funnin'," he protested, his beardless cheeks entirely grave. "I mean it, ma'am. I purely do."

Belle put the pan in the oven, and turning glimpsed a ranch wagon crossing the flats. There was a woman on the high spring seat with a small girl beside her. "I think your mother is coming," she announced.

Kid Beauford got up quickly and peered out the window. "That's her," he said. "Her and Charity. She must of heard about me bein' shot. Wonder how word got to Homestead Valley so soon."

"Bad news always travels fast," Belle said. Then, because she understood how this was going to be, and dreaded it, she said, "If your mother wants you to go home for a while you'd better go."

Kid Beauford shook his head. "We thrashed that out the day I left," he muttered. "I'm seventeen and man-growed. I got a right to take sides, and I'm stickin' with Circle G."

"Of course," Belle agreed, "but there's no reason why you shouldn't spend a little time with your folks, now that you're wounded and not able to ride."

"I can stay here at the ranch and handle a gun lefthanded in case Cameo Kimble should stop by and git fresh with you," the Kid said sullenly. "I saw how he looked at you last time, and I heard him call you honey. That's no fit way for him to talk to you, ma'am — like you was one of Fay Kane's dance girls. No tellin' when that smart-alecky devil will pay you another visit."

Belle lifted a hand to hide the smile she couldn't quite keep back. Kid Beauford's jealousy of Kimble was a standing joke with the Circle G crew. It was comical, and a trifle pathetic. She said, "I'm perfectly capable of defending myself, Kid. You mustn't worry about me."

"It ain't fittin' for a girl like you to be alone while there's so many danged renegades rimmin' around this country," young Beauford insisted. "Look what happened yesterday, you ridin' in after dark with that tough galoot you met on Mormon Ridge. No tellin' what might of happened."

"Lee Ransome may be tough, but he's got a good mannered streak in him," Belle said, remembering how that tall drifter had protected her in the wagon shed. She wondered why he had gone off without saying good-bye, and if she would ever see him again. And would not admit, even to herself, that she couldn't discard the memory of his dark and hungry look as he'd peered at her on Mormon Ridge.

"Ransome," Kid Beauford announced, "is probably another woman chaser just like Kimble."

"No, I don't think so," Belle disagreed. Then, as the wagon rolled into the yard she took the Kid's good arm and ushered him out to the stoop ahead of her.

Mrs. Beauford halted the team and said, "Evenin' Miss Gillum," revealing her implacable dislike in the flat politeness of her voice. Then she looked at her son and compassion warmed her eyes and she cried, "Ezra, boy — you've been hurt!"

Kid Beauford's scrawny face flushed with embarrassment. He said, "Just a busted arm, is all."

"Isn't that enough?" Mrs. Beauford demanded. "If the bullet had gone a few inches to the left you would be dead!"

Kid's six-year-old sister stared at him in

wide-eyed wonderment. "Shotted," she said solemnly. "Ezra has been shotted with a bullet."

Belle smiled at the child, saying, "You're getting to be a big girl, Charity — and pretty as a bug's ear."

"You're pretty too," Charity chirped, showing her dimples. "Maw says that's why Ezra likes you so much."

"Hush, child — hush," Mrs. Beauford commanded. Then she turned to the Kid and said, "I came to take you home, Ezra. You're no good to the Gillums, now that you can't handle a gun."

"That's what I told him," Belle said quietly, ignoring the plain accusation Mrs. Beauford's words implied. "My father will keep him on the payroll until his arm heals. But there's no reason for him not going home with you."

Then, because something in this toil-worn woman's eyes made her feel guilty and ashamed, Belle said impatiently, "Go on, Kid. Go home with your mother."

Whereupon she hurried back into the house.

Lee Ransome had washed up and was sitting on the bunkhouse bench watching the crew unsaddle at the corral when

78

Kimble called from the kitchen doorway, "Come have a cup of coffee."

It sounded, he thought, more like an order than an invitation. The words were all right but there was something in Cameo's tone that sounded wrong. Ransome wondered about it as he walked to the kitchen stoop. This place had a queer feel to it — a menace that got under a man's skin and turned him spooky. He thought: *I'll be hearing queer noises next,* and laughed at himself. But the premonition of impending trouble was like a nagging companion as he went into the kitchen.

Kimble sat at the table with a cup of coffee before him. Now, as Ransome entered, Frenchy Meusette poured a second cup of coffee at a place directly across from Cameo.

"Sit down," Kimble invited. He stirred his coffee, then held the cup in both hands and peered thoughtfully above it. "I knew there was something the matter with that note from Lomax," he announced. "All the way in from town I tried to figure out what it was."

Ransome eyed him narrowly, wondering what was behind this play. Could it be that Kimble was familiar with Lomax's signature and suspected forgery? Or was it something to do with the phrasing — some word or way of speaking that Lomax wouldn't use?

"I knew there was something wrong," Kimble continued. "But I didn't figure it out until just now."

"So?" Ransome asked, and forcing a casualness he didn't feel, sampled his coffee. "Arbuckle at its best," he praised. He turned to Meusette who stood at the stove; "You know how to make it, Frenchy — you sure do."

The cook liked that. He grinned and made a saluting gesture with his hand.

But Kimble was frowning. "You don't spook easy, do you Ransome," he said, as if thinking aloud. "You've been lucky so long it's got to be a habit."

"Good habit to have," Ransome suggested, strongly curious to know what was wrong with the note, yet masking that curiosity in an effort to smother Kimble's suspicion. "A man wouldn't last long if he didn't have Lady Luck's arm around him now and then."

"She hasn't got it around you now," Kimble said scoffingly. "Not if what I think is true."

"Secret?" Ransome asked.

"No, smart boy, it's no secret. I think

you're toting a U.S. marshal's badge." And now Kimble's lips took on a pursey pout as he added harshly, "I think that talk about being a friend of Jim Tarborrow's was a stinkin' lie — just like the note you showed me."

Ransome took another swallow of coffee, using his left hand to lift the cup. He heard the crew washing up at the bunkhouse bench and thought: *I might make it out of here right now, with a little luck.* But then he remembered Frenchy Meusette who was somewhere behind him, and understood how flimsy his chances were.

"What makes you think Lomax lied?" he asked quietly.

"I didn't say Lomax lied," Kimble corrected. "He didn't write the note — nor sign it."

Kimble chuckled. A self-satisfied smile quirked his full, moist lips. But his eyes weren't smiling. They were brittle as blue marbles. "I don't know how you found out about me and Lomax being friends down on the Border," he said. "But I know you picked the wrong man for your fake note. Fred Lomax never learned to write."

So that was it!

Tom Rynning, who'd known about Lomax and Kimble running together three years ago, hadn't checked on Lomax's education. It hadn't occurred to Captain Tom that the man couldn't write, yet now that Ransome thought about it, he supposed that many a rustler sent to prison used an "X" for a signature. An old bitterness, and an old anger rose in him. This was how it always ended for him. No matter how a deal began, the end came down to this.

"You're wrong about the marshal's badge," he muttered, not seeing that it mattered.

"Then what are you doing in this country?" Kimble demanded.

Ransome shrugged. "Like I told you, I'm looking for the thief who framed Jim Tarborrow," he said.

But Kimble didn't believe that. He emphasized his disbelief by shaking his head and saying, "There's more to it than that."

A lot more, Ransome thought morosely. It went all the way back to Texas Junction and Nancy dying in his arms. Five smoky years, a black hell of hate, and a debt of friendship — all these were behind it. They had shaped the pattern of his living, and would one day fashion the manner of his dying. Perhaps this was the day.

As if voicing a half-formed conclusion, Kimble said, "A man would be a sucker to mix into this deal here as a favor to a friend."

"Yeah," Ransome agreed, "which is how I'm feeling right now."

Kimble smiled, shaking his head. "It won't go, kid. You make it sound good, but it won't go. The boys wouldn't believe it if I told them. They'd still think you was a law-dog looking for a train robber."

"How about you?" Ransome asked, not quite sure about this abrupt change in Cameo's manner; and wanting to be sure.

"I'm willing to believe you," Kimble said, and winked. "I never robbed a train."

Meusette loaded the long table with platters containing pan-fried beef, frijoles and corn bread. Then he stepped out to the stoop and sounded supper call on the iron triangle.

Whereupon Kimble said, "Eat hearty, friend. It's on the house."

CHAPTER 6

No Chance at All

The slender crescent of a new moon rimmed Concho Basin's eastern wall. Its fragile glow washed across Tonto Bend, fashioning faint shadow patterns in Ringo Alley where Fay Kane stood with Swamper Smith, the Grand Central Saloon janitor.

"After Tate told him that, Sheriff Sid said he'd take a ride up there tomorrow mornin' for a looksee," Smith reported, his old man's voice barely audible above piano music from the nearby dancehall. "I figgered Cameo ought to know about it."

"He should right away," she agreed. "Will you ride out to Gunman's Camp if I rent you a livery horse?"

"Not me," Smith blurted, backing off. "No ma'am, not me. It ain't safe for a man to rim around that country, day or night. Them Gillums and Tarborrows don't care who they shoot at. They ain't goin' to make no target out of me, by grab!"

Fay Kane stood in thoughtful silence for a moment. With moonlight gilding her blond hair and softly revealing the contours of her heart-shaped face she looked almost girlish. But there was nothing girlish in her thinking, nor in the worry that accompanied that thinking. It was no secret in this town that she was Cameo's woman and now she made no effort to conceal her eager interest in his welfare. "He's got to be warned," she said. "Will you stop by the livery and tell Grogan I'll be wanting a rig in about fifteen minutes?"

"You mean — you're goin' to drive out there by yourself?" Swamper demanded.

Fay nodded, said, "Please go tell Grogan about the rig."

"Sure," Smith agreed, and watching Fay hurry into the Dixie, said forlornly, "If I'd had me a gal like her twenty years ago I wouldn't be swampin' a saloon, by God. I'd own it!"

Moonlight ran across the long mesas to Bootjack Ranch where Doc Smelker wearily washed his hands in a battered pan on the kitchen stoop. "Removing the bullet may not be enough," he announced. "Your brother lost too much blood."

"But he's got a chance, ain't he?" Tate Tarborrow demanded.

The young medico nodded. "A bare chance," he muttered, then added in a thoroughly disillusioned voice, "A bare chance to survive so he can shoot and be shot at again. I never saw such a lawless country."

A Bootjack rider cursed. "We had law plenty the day they sent young Jim to Yuma," he said. "Big Bart Gillum law."

Sam Tarborrow's wife came rushing out to the stoop. "Come quick, Doc," she pleaded. "I think he's dyin' — don't let him, Doc — don't let my Sam die!"

Doc hurried inside and the woman went with him.

A man over in the shadows said, "Sam was a real nice feller."

Then, as the woman screamed hysterically, Tate Tarborrow began pounding a stoop post with his fist. "Them goddam Gillums!" he muttered, and kept repeating it, like a chant.

The moon rose higher, burnishing weather-carved castles atop Rimrock Reef. It dropped down the steep slants to Gunman's Camp where Lee Ransome stood at the kitchen sink soaking the bruised and swollen knuckles of his right hand in a pan of hot water. Frenchy Meusette, long since finished with his dishwashing, had gone to join the bunkhouse poker game.

The little cook was a queer one, Ransome reflected. Queer inside and out. Frenchy had fetched him a bottle of liniment and insisted, by solicitous gesture and wordless mumbling, that his hand be soaked in the hot water which he provided. Yet a few hours ago Meusette had shot down an unarmed comrade as mercilessly as a butcher slaughtering a beef.

There'd been little conversation at the supper table. When Hack Benson inquired about burying Surdine, Cameo had said the body would be taken to town in the morning. Whereupon Joe Tanner asked how Red's death could be explained to Sheriff Baffert.

"In a way you'd never guess," Cameo had said slyly. And then he chuckled as if enjoying a secret joke.

There was another odd one, Ransome thought now. It was difficult to classify Cameo Kimble, for the man possessed a veritable hodgepodge of conflicting characteristics. He could be gracious and charming, when the occasion called for it; yet he was brutal to the core, and merciless as a coiled rattlesnake. Cameo hadn't mentioned the fake note, nor the fact that he'd chosen a new foreman. He had praised Frenchy's cooking, and backed his words by taking second helpings of everything. The man was a riddle, and utterly unpredictable.

Ransome had given most of his attention to Society Slim, studying the ex-cavalry officer and endeavoring to see him as a road agent. Except that he was tall, and had a pair of gloves in his hip pocket, Slim didn't seem to fit the robber role at all. Slim might be a first class fighting man, as Kimble had bragged, despite his cultured voice and mannerisms — a gentleman turned tough by remorse and disillusionment. But he didn't have the look of a thief.

According to Jim Tarborrow the masked bandit had worn a yellow slicker which concealed his clothing, so there was no way of telling whether he'd been neat about his apparel, as Slim was, or careless as most men were. Young Tarborrow hadn't been sure about the bandit's eyes.

"I was watchin' his gun, wantin' to see it waggle enough so's I could make a play," he had explained.

There seemed no means of identifying the robber except for the fact that he'd worn gloves on a warm day.

I'll watch Slim tomorrow, Ransome thought, and examined his hand. The swelling had diminished. He flexed his fingers and felt only a slight soreness that matched the soreness of his ribs where Surdine had hit him. Going out to the stoop Ransome dried his hand on Kimble's private towel and glanced toward the bunkhouse.

For a moment, as he contemplated the long structure, Ransome was mildly surprised. Then abruptly all his senses roused to razor-edged sharpness, and apprehension was like a cold breeze blowing against the back of his neck. The bunkhouse was dark!

Kimble and his hardcase crew weren't playing poker now. There wasn't a sign of them anywhere. But he knew they hadn't departed, nor gone to bed. And although he couldn't see them, he understood exactly what they were doing. They were watching him — watching a living target!

The conviction that this was so — that he was marked for slaughter — prowled Lee Ransome's mind like a cat in a dark alley. It clawed at his stomach and was a clutching tightness in his throat; it chilled him so that he shivered, yet perspiration dripped from his armpits. He tried to discard it; to tell himself that imagination had got the best of him. But the awareness clung to him like a cloak and one idea dominated his thinking: they had him in a tight, sure trap.

Desperately, as a man contemplating a familiar yet fearsome predicament, Ransome peered across the faintly moonlit yard. Were they in the bunkhouse? Or in the clotted shadows of the wagon shed? Or in the pool of darkness at the windmill water tank?

He glanced at the corral, identifying his roan gelding which stood within the slatted shadow pattern of the gate. He thought: *If the roan was twenty-five feet closer, and saddled, there might be a chance.*

It occurred to Ransome now that his only chance for survival was through the doorway behind him. If he could get back into the cabin and go through a window he might make it into timber. He'd be afoot, of course, and fair game for mounted riders. There wasn't much likelihood of eluding a concentrated search, but any chance at all was better than walking into waiting guns he couldn't see.

He was turning toward the lamp-lit doorway when Cameo Kimble called sharply, "Come on out, Ransome. I've figured out a chore for you to do — your first chore as foreman."

Ransome faced the yard, seeing no sign of Kimble, or of the crew. A gentle breeze, drifting down from Rimrock Reef, stirred the windmill to brief clanking. When that passed there was no sound at all. The silence ran on until the pressure of it was like a vice squeezing Lee Ransome's nerves; until suspense greased the palms of his hands with perspiration and put a grinding ache at the pit of his stomach.

And still there was no sign nor sound of movement in the yard.

This, Ransome understood, was Kimble's idea of sport — to play with a man. Cameo had a feline streak in him; a sadistic taste for subtle torture. He had proved that by handing Surdine's gun to Meusette instead of shooting Red himself. Kimble had enjoyed the spectacle of Surdine's frantic fear. Now he wanted to watch the disintegration of another man's courage. And he would take whatever time was necessary to accomplish the chore.

That understanding, backed by the memory of Kimble saying that he didn't spook easy, prompted Lee Ransome to a rash decision. There didn't seem to be a chance of survival here, but there might be a way to postpone the shooting, if he played his cards correctly. So thinking, Ransome took out his Durham sack. Methodically shaping a cigarette, he asked, "Where you at, Cameo?"

Kimble chuckled, that sound seeming to come from the bunkhouse doorway. "Over here in the dark," Cameo said. "It sure is lonesome."

"Same here," Hack Benson called from behind the windmill tank. "I never been so goddam lonesome in all my borned days."

And Joe Tanner's rasping voice came from the wagon shed, saying, "Me too."

Society Slim, Ransome guessed, was somewhere behind the cabin, which made the ring complete.

"What's the chore?" Ransome inquired.

"I've decided you should go to town with Red," Kimble announced, "so Sheriff Baffert won't ask a lot of questions."

As if eager to make that meaning wholly clear, Joe Tanner explained quickly, "We're goin' to tell the star-packer that you and Red shot each other in a shootin' scrape. We'll tell it like you killed Red, then died of the slugs he put into you before he dropped. It'll make a real nice story."

That reminded Ransome of this reedy rider's question at the supper table, and how Kimble had said: "In a way you'd never guess." Cameo had thought this out ahead of time. He had a mania for scheming, for approaching a goal by indirection. . . .

"Red disliked lawdogs somethin' terrible," Benson commented, his heavy voice booming across the yard like a bull's bellow. "Especially U.S. marshals on the hunt for train robbers."

It occurred to Ransome that he could prove he wasn't a marshal by merely showing the Ranger badge in his pants pocket. But the futility of such revelation came to him at once. Cameo Kimble wasn't choosy about the type of badge-toter he had trapped. The important thing was to eliminate a lawman who might cause him trouble. It was, Ransome admitted, a perfect solution, from Kimble's standpoint. And Cameo was a schemer who believed in playing all the angles.

"How you feel now, sucker?" Kimble called tauntingly.

Ransome had stood with the tapered cigarette in his fingers. Now he raised it to his lips, licked the paper's edge and stuck the complete cigarette between his lips. Cameo, he reflected, wouldn't be satisfied to end this deal without some manifestation of fear, or stupefied despair. While he was waiting for that there might be a break — some trivial shift in the odds that would give a man a fighting chance. There were a few high clouds in the sky; if one of them drifted in front of the moon for a moment he could jump off this lamp-lit stoop without making a plain target.

Ransome wondered about Meusette. Even though Kimble had said he was lonesome, Frenchy was probably with him in the bunkhouse. Society Slim, he felt sure, was behind the cabin. *Probably watching the window,* Ransome thought. Covertly calculating the distance he would have to run in order to turn the cabin's south corner he estimated it at not more than ten or twelve feet.

"Ain't you got nothin' to say?" Hack Benson boomed.

Ransome thumbed a match to flame and held it to his cigarette. He flipped the match away, took a deep drag of smoke and allowed it to filter slowly from his nostrils. Finally he said, "I think you stink, Benson. You smell like a goddam sheep-herder to me. Did you work for the Daggs brothers north of the Rim before you came here?"

That question seemed to stump Hack, and in this interval of silence Ransome contemplated the moves he must make in order to round the cabin wall. He would choose a moment when someone was talking, preferably Kimble. He would toss his cigarette out into the yard, hoping that the momentary distraction of its glowing arc would allow him to get under motion before they noticed what he was doing. The rest of it, of course, would depend on luck — and the accuracy of the first frenzied shooting. If he got around behind the cabin there'd be just one gun to face as he ran into the timber.

No use thinking beyond that, Ransome reflected with a gambler's fatalism. There'd been other times when the odds were stacked too high; times when even the hope of survival had seemed silly as a drunkard's dream. Yet on each of those occasions Lady Luck had held her arm around him. Perhaps she would now. . . .

But in the next moment, as he waited for the talk to start again, there was a step in the doorway behind him and Society Slim said complainingly, "Let's get it over with, Cameo. I much prefer to play poker."

Lee Ransome knew then that he was doomed. No chance now to make a dash behind the house; no fighting chance at all!

Cameo Kimble's chuckle ran softly from the bunkhouse shadows. "Perhaps Ransome would like to play poker also," he suggested. "How about it, sucker?"

Ransome shrugged. There seemed to be no point in further pretense. But some stubborn, deep-rooted pride kept him from revealing the hopelessness he felt. "Sure, Cameo. I'll play some poker."

He eased off the stoop and started toward the bunkhouse at a leisurely gait and wondered how many steps he'd take before they started shooting. There was no way of guessing who would start it, but if Kimble fired first there would be a chance to slam one shot at him, using muzzle flare for a target.

One shot before he went down. . . .

Keeping his right hand close to holster, Ransome took another step, and another. Kimble, he understood, was playing with him again; giving him the silent treatment. The lonely, lost-dog treatment that could crush a man's morale. Killing him wasn't enough for Cameo; the dirty son had to make his victim feel the awful loneliness of his last few minutes on earth.

Perspiration felt sleety cold against Ransome's skin. He had an almost overwhelming urge to call out — to curse or plead or loose a piercing rebel yell; anything to break the sense of utter aloneness.

This, he knew, was how Red Surdine had felt just before he died. It was what had prodded him to that frantic, futile run toward the wagon shed. And now Cameo Kimble was waiting to see the same sorry spectacle again.

Ransome cursed softly and continued his methodical march across the yard. All hope of survival had drained out of him leaving one dismal purpose in its wake — to have his shot at Cameo Kimble. He was halfway across the yard when a horse nickered in the corral, and this equine call was answered from somewhere in the timber. Ransome halted. The rhythmic thump of a trotting horse came faintly from the tree-shadowed road, and with it was the unmistakable sound of wheels clattering over stones.

Joe Tanner heard it also for he called, "Somebody comin' in a rig."

A long sigh slid from Ransome's lips as the tension ran out of him. Here, he thought with swift-rising hope, might be the break he needed. . . .

Kimble ordered, "Slim, you keep an eye on Ransome," and came out of the bunkhouse with a gun in his hand. "Wonder who in hell it can be."

Ransome grinned, watching Tanner and

Benson emerge from the shadows. The oncoming rig had disrupted this deal completely. Kimble had played his lost-dog game a trifle too long; he'd given Lady Luck a chance to operate.

Then, as the rig rattled into the yard and Ransome recognized the driver's moonlit face, he almost laughed out loud. His luck wasn't a lady, strictly speaking, but Fay Kane would do until a real lady came along!

Kimble went to the buggy at once, helping Fay down and demanding, "What's wrong, honey?"

Ransome recalled that Cameo had used the same term of intimacy with the hotel waitress, and wondered if he also used it with Belle Gillum.

"Swamper Smith heard Tate Tarborrow tell Baffert that none of his bunch raided Circle G," she reported. "Tate said it must've been your riders that did it, and Baffert said he would take a look at the tracks tomorrow morning to see where they led to. I thought you should know, in case Tate was telling the truth."

In the momentary silence that followed, she asked, "Was he lying, Cameo?"

"Sure," Kimble said. Then a new thought struck him and he turned to Joe

Tanner demanding, "Was Red here yesterday evening?"

Tanner shook his head, and Hack Benson announced, "Red didn't git in till around midnight. We thought he was with you."

"So that's it!" Kimble exclaimed angrily. "Red shot up Circle G by himself. The goddam fool might've killed Belle instead of the cook!"

"That would have been a terrible joke on you, wouldn't it, Cameo," Fay murmured with mock sympathy. Then she inquired, "Well, aren't you going to ask me to have a glass of water at least?"

"Of course, honey; of course," Kimble said, remembering his manners. "Frenchy, put on the coffeepot," he ordered and, bowing gallantly, offered Fay his arm.

She was accompanying him toward the house when she peered at Ransome and exclaimed, "Lee — Lee Ransome! What in the world are you doing here?"

Ransome grinned, remembering how this blond woman had once attracted men with romantic notions in Texas Junction. He said, "I'm glad to see you, Fay," and glancing obliquely at Kimble, added, "Real glad for a fact."

Kimble didn't like this deal and showed

it by stepping between them and saying gruffly, "Just forget you saw Ransome tonight. Forget all about it."

"Why?" Fay demanded.

"I'll explain it later," Kimble said impatiently and escorted her toward the house.

Ransome smiled thinly, understanding why Kimble resented this meeting. Fay couldn't know it, but she had spoken to a dead man — a man who was supposed to have been shot by Red Surdine several hours ago. It complicated things immensely, having Fay see him alive at this late hour. And now, as Ransome heard Society Slim greet Fay, he noticed how close the rig was. How invitingly close. . . .

Instantly then, Lee Ransome knew what he was going to do. Or what he was going to attempt to do. Joe Tanner and Hack Benson, who had drifted over by the wagon shed, were discussing Red's one man raid. Frenchy Meusette was in the kitchen now and Society Slim was conversing with Fay Kane in gentlemanly fashion. Ransome thought urgently: *There'll never be a better time to try it!*

Convinced that this was so, he eased a step closer to the rig, observing that the reins were draped over the dashboard and that the front wheels were cramped exactly right for boarding the buggy. Then he flung himself forward and leaped into the rig. Grasping reins and whip he lashed the spooked horse into plunging motion; he whirled the rig past the water tank in a skidding turn and heard Joe Tanner's warning yell a split-second before the first bullet whanged past him.

The rest of it was a frantic, frenzied nightmare of noise and confusion. A bullet ricocheted crazily from some metal part of the buggy as Ransome guided the galloping horse into a rocky, wheel-rutted road that curved into timber. He heard the wicked whine of close-flying slugs and felt the sharp hot bite of one he didn't hear; one that clawed his left arm with a violence that made him drop the reins.

The rig, bouncing and careening wildly, was almost to the timber's belt of deep shadows when Ransome retrieved the reins. His wounded arm ached throbbingly, but it wasn't broken. The bullet, he guessed, had sliced along the muscle between wrist and elbow.

One gun was still firing back there in the yard, its bullets falling short somewhere behind him. He thought happily: *I made it, by God — I made it!*

And because there was in him now a

gambler's exuberance on winning a high-stake game, Ransome loosed an exultant, long-drawn rebel yell.

But presently, as the road angled up a timbered slope, he understood that he must leave the rig. Kimble and his men were probably saddling up right now and they would be riding fresh horses that could overtake him in a matter of minutes. . . .

So thinking, Ransome jumped to the ground. Peering about for a likely place to make a stand in case he was discovered, he glimpsed a windfall some twenty yards north of the road. He was hunkered there, gun in hand, when four riders galloped past. He caught a brief glimpse of Cameo Kimble's face briefly revealed in a shaft of tree-filtered moonlight, and heard him shout, "We'll swing around and get ahead of him."

Ransome grinned. Cameo was still playing it safe. Even with three guns to back him, Kimble wanted to set a sure-thing ambush. The boss of Gunman's Camp was so full of tinhorn tricks they ran out his ears, Ransome reflected. But this one was all in his favor, for it would postpone discovery of his absence in the rig. Easing out to the road he moved into a shaft of moonlight and examined his bullet-gouged arm. The wound wasn't more than two inches long, nor very deep; but it was bleeding profusely and now a numbness ran all the way down to his fingers.

"Ought to fix a tourniquet," Ransome muttered, and listened to the diminishing rumor of running horses. It would take those four gunhawks a little time to circle around the rig and set their ambush. He smiled, thinking how surprised Cameo would be when he found the rig unoccupied. After that they would start hunting him. And because he was afoot they'd find him. Not tonight, perhaps, but tomorrow. Eventually they'd ride him down.

Whereupon Ransome turned and walked hurriedly back the way he had come. The thing he had in mind was risky, but it was the last thing they'd expect him to do. That, and a little luck, might mean the difference between living and dying. . . .

CHAPTER 7

Target in the Moonlight

Fay Kane stood on the kitchen stoop with Frenchy Meusette and watched the men ride away at a dust-boiling run. What, she wondered, was all this about? There seemed no rhyme nor reason to it. One moment Lee Ransome had seemed to be a member of Cameo's crew; then he had grabbed her livery rig and everyone started shooting at him. It just didn't make sense.

When Frenchy turned back into the kitchen she went with him, asking, "Why did Ransome run off?"

She couldn't comprehend Meusette's excited jabbering, nor understand the motions he made with his hands. He pointed to his vest pocket and uttered a gurgling moan that sounded like "Garmul."

Fay shook her head, unable to guess his meaning. She said, "Never mind, Frenchy. How about fixing me something to eat? I'm starved."

For a time then, while Meusette stoked up the fire and prepared a meal for her, Fay Kane thought about the old days in Texas Junction when she'd known Lee Ransome. "So long ago," she mused. "So terribly long ago."

Not in years, but in the change those years had produced. . . .

She had been stranded in Texas Junction after a variety show went broke; a twenty-year-old girl with stars in her eyes and a burning ambition to become a great actress. She had accepted a job at the Bon Ton Saloon, singing her heart out for small wages and saving for the stake that would one day take her to a concert stage in San Francisco or New York.

Oh, she'd had big dreams then; big ambitions. And the untarnished pride that went with them. But as the months went by the dreams faded, taking some of her pride with them. And there were the men — the eager, coaxing, smooth-talking men.

Lee Ransome had been city marshal then, a strict, unsmiling man who made toughs toe the line. Fay smiled reflectively, recalling how he had pistol-whipped a brazen bull of a teamster who'd invaded her hotel room with lustful intentions. He had been like a crazy man, that teamster, a passion-prodded studhorse of a man. She had been horribly frightened when Lee Ransome came barging into the room, and so appreciative afterward that she kissed him. But the marshal had shrugged off her worshipful admiration, saying, "It was just part of the job I'm paid for doing."

Fay marveled at the difference the years had made. There were no stars in her eyes now, no burning ambition to be a great singer. She owned a dancehall, and a half interest in this ranch, and was known as Cameo Kimble's woman. A cynical smile pouted her lips as she compared these possessions with the discarded dreams. There wasn't much pride left, either. Cameo had taken that, along with everything else she'd given him. . . .

Frenchy Meusette placed a plate of warmed-up beef and frijoles before her. He was turning to get the coffeepot when Lee Ransome eased through the doorway with a gun in his hand and said, "Don't move, Frenchy. I'm going to take your gun."

"Your arm is bleeding!" Fay exclaimed, staring at his torn, blood-soaked sleeve.

Ransome ignored her, not taking his eyes off Meusette as he stepped across the kitchen. The little cook stood rigidly still while Ransome took his gun. But his brown eyes weren't submissive; they held a malevolent glitter as Ransome prodded him toward the doorway.

"What's this rumpus about?" Fay demanded.

Ransome grinned at her, observing that she wore her blond hair in the same high-coiled fashion she'd worn it in the Bon Ton. But her heart-shaped face was fuller and her eyes no longer held the animated sparkle of a stage-struck girl. He wondered if she could still sing *Sweet Alice Ben Bolt* in a lilting, soft-toned voice that made a lump come into a man's throat.

"Why did you run off in my rig?" Fay insisted.

"Because I didn't want to take Red Surdine's place as your boyfriend's foreman," Ransome said.

"Red's place? What happened to him?"

"He's dead," Ransome reported. Prodding Meusette out to the stoop he dropped Frenchy's gun in the water bucket and ordered, "Go saddle my horse and be quick about it."

Fay followed them across the yard. "I wish you'd tell me what's going on here," she complained. "It doesn't make sense."

"No time for talk," Ransome muttered, watching Meusette catch his roan gelding and lead it from the corral.

"Your arm needs a bandage," Fay insisted. "It's still bleeding."

"No time for that either," Ransome said. He canted his head, listening for a moment. Then he took off his neckerchief and handed it to Fay, saying, "A tourniquet would help."

The irony of this made him smile. Here was Kimble's cook saddling his horse and Kimble's woman binding his wounded arm, while the boss of Gunman's Camp was out in the timber gunning for him. Like Fay said, it didn't make sense.

When she had the tourniquet tied Ransome said, "Thanks, ma'am. Thanks a lot."

Fay stood close, smiling up at him now and saying softly, "I haven't forgotten the night that loco teamster insisted on having his way with me."

She looked small, and wistful and girlish again, out here in the moonlight. "Maybe the teamster wasn't so loco," Ransome mused. "Maybe his eyesight was better than mine."

Then he turned to supervise the saddling, and when it was done, mounted quickly and gave Fay a farewell salute as he loped out of the yard.

★ ★ ★

Cameo Kimble peered at the empty rig and cursed.

"The smart-alecky son must of took to the brush!" Hack Benson blurted. "He's done give us the slip!"

"A sly fox, that Ransome," Society Slim remarked.

But Joe Tanner, holding the livery horse's headstall, suggested, "Maybe he fell out of the rig, Cameo. All them slugs couldn't of missed hitting him. I bet he's layin' alongside the road somewhere dead as a mackerel."

That possibility pleased Cameo. "I hope you're right," he said, smiling now. "Take the rig back to Fay, but don't tell her anything, Joe. Women talk too goddam much. If you find Ransome's body fire three shots. Otherwise ride towards Rimrock Reef trail till you meet me."

"What about the tracks Red made ridin' from Circle G?" Tanner asked. "Hadn't we better mess up that sign before Baffert gits there in the morning?"

Kimble nodded. "But I want Ransome first," he said impatiently. "I want that bastard spraddled out nice and peaceful beside Red in the wagon."

He turned to the others, saying, "Slim,

you and Hack work back on both sides of the road while I cover Rimrock Reef. If Ransome is able to walk he'll head for town. Be sure he doesn't get past you."

"He wouldn't use the road, would he?" Hack Benson asked. "Why don't the three of us fan out across the trail which is where a man on foot would most likely go?"

But Cameo shook his head. "Ransome is just smart enough to take the road, figuring we wouldn't expect him to. I brought him in by the trail and that's the logical way for him to go out. So he'll most likely take the road, figuring to cross us up."

Cameo chuckled, proud of his strategy. "It takes a fox to catch a fox," he bragged, and watching Tanner turn the rig around, called, "Keep your eyes open for a corpse, Joe. That's what we want — a nice quiet corpse."

Then he rode through sparse timber toward the base of Rimrock Reef. Joe might be right, Kimble thought, but he wasn't depending on it. Ransome was a slick one, and lucky enough to wiggle out of this alive. Anger and apprehension prodded Kimble at thought of the Texan telling what he'd seen and heard tonight. Especially the part about Red Surdine raiding Circle G. That could spoil every-thing.

Kimble cursed, thinking what Red's raid and Ransome's escape might cost him. If Big Bart found out about it there'd be no use explaining. Gillum would call him a liar; and Belle, who'd often expressed her opinion of his crew, would hold him directly responsible for the cook's death.

Because he wanted Belle Gillum more than he'd ever wanted any woman, Kimble cursed his dead foreman. Yet it was Ransome who would really spoil things, if they were spoiled. He thought: *I should've chopped him down sooner.* But there'd seemed to be no need for hurry. They'd had Ransome dead to rights. Only Fay's arrival had furnished Ransome his chance for escape. Thinking of that now, Kimble muttered, "Damn her swivel-hipped soul to hell!"

She had been a goddam nuisance these past few weeks, he reflected; always talking about marriage, and how she would like to sell the dancehall and live at the ranch. He had tried to convince her that he wasn't a marrying man — that she should take Sid Baffert if she wanted a husband. Cameo grinned, thinking how meekly Sid had courted her. Like a hound dog waiting for a handout. Hell, that was no way to get a woman.

Halting to listen, Kimble heard only a remote rumor of wheels to the north. Joe, he guessed, hadn't found anything, for the rig was nearly to the yard now. He rode up the steep chute-like trail at a scrambling run. Even though he didn't expect Ransome to come this way he might spot him from the rim and thus know exactly where the chase should be concentrated. . . .

At about this same moment Lee Ransome sat his horse in tree-dappled shadows a mile south of Gunman's Camp. There was, he supposed, only one trail across Rimrock Reef. Kimble and his crew must have discovered the empty wagon by now, which meant they'd be fanning out to hunt him, believing he was afoot. And they would be endeavoring to guess which way a man would walk. The trail, most likely, for it was a shortcut to town. But Kimble might be smart enough to outguess a man — might choose to guard the least logical avenue of escape.

Ransome shrugged, seeing no sure method of making the right choice. With a gambler's fatalism he drew a silver dollar from his pocket, said, "Heads I take the trail," and flipped the coin. It came up tails.

Riding at an angle that would take him toward the road, Ransome halted at frequent intervals to listen. This was the danger zone. Cameo and his men would be somewhere in this vicinity which was less than three miles from Gunman's Camp. If they'd elected to watch the road he would be spotted the first time he crossed a clearing. And there was one directly ahead of him.

Halting just inside the last fringe of trees, Ransome scouted the shadows beyond a bald, moonlit bench. It occurred to him that he could ride north from here with no danger of ambush. But there was a throbbing ache in his arm above the tourniquet, and a wooden numbness below it. The wound needed a medico's attention; it should be properly washed and bandaged before infection set in. And that meant a trip to town.

It was near midnight now with a breeze stirring the high-branched pines to gentle sighing. Ransome shivered, and buttoned his denim riding jacket. There was a hint of approaching winter in the chill breeze; it reminded him that this was the farthest north he'd ever been. He took another long look at the far side of the clearing, a sense of ambush so strong in him now that he drew his gun.

As always, at times like this Ransome craved a cigarette. But he couldn't risk it. That, he thought, was what the gunhawk game did to a man; made him afraid to take the frugal pleasure of a smoke. *A sucker's game,* he reflected dismally and knew he'd had his fill of it. Remembering that Kimble had called him a sucker, he said, "That's what I am. A shot-up sucker riding a dead man's saddle."

The moon was high now, brighter than it had been back in the yard. And those clouds he'd hoped might mask it were banked above Concho Rim. They would be no help to him this night. He calculated the road's location and guessed it lay just beyond the next low ridge. But it might be farther, depending on the angles of its turning. Kimble and his crew could be over there now, or they might be strung out between Rimrock Reef and the road. It occurred to Ransome that he wasn't sure of anything.

Then he grinned and thought: *One thing.* Except for Fay Kane's arrival he would be dead now. There was no doubt in his mind about that. She had saved his bacon. That much he was sure of. And, ironically, it was Red's raid on Circle G which had brought her to Gunman's Camp. Fate, he reflected, fashioned queer patterns. He was thinking about that as he eased his horse out of the timber. A man never knew which part of the pattern might affect him later on, nor what his part in it would be.

Ransome rode at a walk, scanning the yonder shadows and listening for some telltale sound of movement. Once across this clearing he would have a fair chance of making it to town. The roan was rested, and because he had a quarter strain of Thoroughbred in him, could outrun any cold-blooded horse in the country.

Midway across the bald bench now, Ransome sat easier in his saddle, believing he was going to make it unobserved. Kimble, he supposed, had pulled his men back toward the trail.

Not as smart as he looks, Ransome decided. And at this exact instant a gun opened up directly ahead of him. . . .

The wicked whine of the bullet came a split-second before the explosion, so close to his head that Ransome dodged instinctively and thus threw the roan off stride. The swift change of direction saved him from a second bullet which was wide by several feet. He slammed a shot toward the yonder muzzle flare and as another gun

115

exploded farther to the south, whirled his horse into a pivoting turn. No chance now to cross the clearing. They had him cut off from two angles.

There was just one thing left to do: run in the only direction left to run — northward. And because each close-flying slug set his back muscles to crawling, Ransome cursed the moonlight which made him so plain a target.

A target they wouldn't miss. . . .

Yet it was upwards of an hour, with Ransome playing a desperate, dodging game of hide and seek, before a bullet ripped his right thigh. He thought they had him then, for he'd mistaken a box canyon for a pass. But the brave-hearted roan outran them.

Afterward, near daybreak, two riders came so close to his thicket hiding place that Ransome recognized Hack Benson's voice. The moon was down and they passed without investigating the thicket. Ransome knew then that his luck still held. But because he was cold and weak and worn out he took little satisfaction in it.

CHAPTER 8

"Weak as a Gutted Calf"

Luke Beauford rested his team at the crest of the divide south of Homestead Valley. The wagon was empty, save for a crate of eggs to be bartered at the Mercantile, but Beauford always halted here for a last look at his land.

A pleasing sight at any time of day, but especially so now; with early morning sunlight washing across his alfalfa patch and tinting it to a rich viridian, it was purely beautiful to Luke Beauford. He couldn't see all of his cattle from here, but there were sixty-seven head grazing in the pine-bordered pasture and half of them were fat steers that would bring top prices. A hundred rainless days had turned the round-about range tawny and tinder dry so that his few irrigated acres were like a lush oasis against the parched sprawl of country.

Luke Beauford's knobby, sun-blackened face showed a reflective smile as he recalled how his two nearest neighbors had once jibed at him for sinking his well so deep, and casing it. "A needless waste of money," they'd scoffed. "You can get all the water you'll ever need with a dug well at twenty feet." Now those two places, which they no longer owned, were hardscrabble line camps with scarcely enough water for drinking purposes.

Beauford clucked to his team and drove on through the pass. A frugal, God-fearing man who abided by the Ten Commandments, he had spent seven years getting a foothold in Concho Basin — seven toilsome years of scrimping and saving and working for wages at odd jobs until he had what he wanted. Now, because he owned the best water supply in the valley, Cameo Kimble was trying to bamboozle him out of it; was using scalawag tricks to scare him into selling.

Last week a pair of Kimble's linecamp riders had used Luke's windmill for target practice on their way home from town late at night. Day before yesterday they'd run a bunch of big steers through his fence and deliberately trampled an acre of alfalfa on the pretext of retrieving the stampeded stock.

"But they'll not scare me out," Beauford

said stubbornly, repeating the exact words he'd told his wife on numerous occasions. When the Gillum-Tarborrow feud ended there'd be law and order in this country again. Range wars didn't last forever. One side or the other would go under eventually. A peaceful man could wait it out if he refused to be frightened off his land.

Beauford frowned, thinking how tedious and terrifying the waiting could be. Especially at night with hate-prodded raiders crossing his unfenced section; with Kimble's drunken renegades howling like Apaches as they galloped past his place. It was bad for Ruth and little Charity, being scared out of their wits in the middle of the night. And even daytimes, when he was away from the house. But it wouldn't be so bad now with Ezra home. Even though the boy wasn't in fit shape to help with the work, he could keep the womenfolk company.

The broken arm might teach Ezra something, Luke thought, recalling how he'd done his best to explain why a peaceable man couldn't take sides in the Gillum-Tarborrow feud. But Ezra wouldn't listen then. He had ridden off, proud as a tom turkey, with a new gun in a new holster and hired himself out to Big Bart Gillum.

"Girl crazy," his mother called him, "his head so full of silly notions that he can't see she's just teasin' him on."

Ezra had a case on the Gillum girl, all right, but there was more to it than that, Luke guessed. A hot-blooded young buck just naturally liked to fight for the pure excitement of fighting. He had been that way himself as a boy back in Missouri. But he'd got over it quick when he met Ruth, whose father was a Methodist minister. The old clergyman wouldn't let him come near the house until he worked a steady job for a year and had no fighting at all.

Beauford smiled, remembering those romantic times. Ruth had tamed him for a fact; she'd taught him house manners and got him into the habit of asking the blessing at supper table. There'd been some troublesome times when sickness came and money was hard to come by; but they'd been happy regardless, until this range war had turned things haywire.

Presently, as his wagon rumbled across Manana Mesa's long flat top, Beauford glimpsed a rider briefly skylined off to the east. Soon after that another horseman crossed a pine-bordered meadow south of him. This was Kimble's range and Beauford thought: *They must be startin' their gather early.* He shrugged, thinking it wouldn't take them long to get the job done. It was a standing joke in Concho Basin that Cameo owned more horses than he did cattle. That wasn't true, of course, but Kimble controlled a big smear of range for the small number of cows which wore his Heart K brand.

Beauford was driving down the long slope into Squaw Canyon when Joe Tanner rode out of the brush. Joe's eyes were bloodshot and a scowl rutted his pock-pitted cheeks as he rode up close to the wagon, peering into it as if seeking contra-band cargo. He looked, Luke thought, like he'd been helling around in town all night.

"You see anybody back yonder?" Tanner demanded.

Beauford despised the men on Kimble's payroll only slightly less than he despised Cameo. He resented this tough's arrogance and showed it by remaining silent.

"Speak up!" Tanner ordered crankily. "You see anyone north of here?"

Beauford nodded, but he didn't speak. He just sat there looking at Tanner as if smelling a bad odor.

"Listen you goddam plow jockey!" Tanner shouted. "Don't look down your scabby nose at me when I'm askin' you a question. Who'd you see?"

"Too far off to tell," Beauford said.

"Was he a tall galoot on a roan horse?"

Beauford shook his head. "Saw two of 'em," he drawled with deliberate slowness. "One was ridin' a bald-faced sorrel and the other a black, or maybe a brown."

"Hack and Society Slim," Tanner muttered. He peered off across the canyon at a rider who came out of the tumbled boulders over there. Without shifting his squint-eyed gaze he pulled a Winchester from its scabbard. Anticipation tightened his beard-stubbled face; it pressed his lips to a thin, vicious line so that Beauford, watching him, thought: *He's a killer in his heart — a natural borned killer.*

Tanner cursed and relaxed and watched the rider's slow progress along the canyon, saying, "That's Cameo."

"Who you fellers huntin'?" Beauford inquired.

"A drifter named Ransome," Tanner muttered. "He's wounded."

"What'd he do?"

That question seemed to puzzle Tanner. He didn't reply for a moment. Finally he said, "Ransome killed Red Surdine," whereupon he rode along the slope with his Winchester cradled across his arm.

Beauford clucked to his team, taking satisfaction in the news that Surdine was dead. "Good riddance," he mused.

Kimble's foreman had scared Ruth half out of her wits a couple weeks ago. He'd been riding past the yard with Hack Benson when the dog rushed out to bark at them. Surdine fired three shots, killing the dog with two bullets. But the first one had smashed into the front stoop a foot from where little Charity sat playing with her doll.

Beauford grimaced, recalling how Ruth had talked to him that evening when he got back from a trip to town. She had never been much of a hand to go into hysterics but she'd been purely wrought up that time. She had sobbed and pleaded, wanting him to sell out; saying that Concho Basin was no fit place for decent folks to live. Afterward she had accused him of cherishing his land above his family. A bad time, that had been. Awful bad. But he'd refused to leave, regardless. . . .

Beauford wondered about the drifter who'd killed Surdine. The poor devil wouldn't stand much chance with Kimble's bunch after him. Especially if he was wounded. Luke shook his head, thinking how it would be to dodge around through the hills with gunhawks closing in like a pack of hounds. It gave a man the crawling creeps just thinking about it.

He was out of the canyon and past the Circle G fork of the road when he met Sheriff Baffert. "Out a trifle early for a town dude, ain't you Sid?" Beauford greeted.

Baffert grinned, knowing there was no real malice in this homesteader's sarcasm. "What's new up your way, Luke?"

"Nothin' yet, but there will be, startin' tomorrow," Beauford announced. "I'm goin' to buy enough bob wire to run a drift fence clean across the west side of my section."

Surprise widened Baffert's eyes. "How come?" he asked.

"Them west linecamp toughs been pushin' Kimble's stuff my way all summer," Beauford muttered. "Day before yesterday they run a jag of big steers into my alfalfa patch and tramped an acre of it down on purpose before they left. Maybe a drift fence'll keep 'em off my land."

Baffert eased his big-paunched body in the saddle. He took a cigar from his vest pocket and eyed it thoughtfully for a moment before saying, "Kimble might not like that. Neither will Tarborrow or Gillum. They want the country kept open range, which seems reasonable. Fencin' an alfalfa patch is one thing, Luke, but stringin' bob wire across a whole section. . . ."

"No law agin it, is there?" Beauford demanded.

Baffert shook his head. "No law agin a man stickin' his foot into a bear trap, neither. But it might prove painful, Luke — tol'able painful."

"Well, I ain't goin' to just sit on my pants and see my winter feed bein' tromped into the ground," Beauford said stubbornly. "I've told you the tricks Kimble has been playin' and you've done nothin' to stop him. Not a thing."

Baffert shrugged. "It would take a force of five or ten deputies to stop drunk cowboys from shootin' at windmills and trespassin' on private property," he explained quietly. "I used to have three deputies but two of 'em went to work for Gillum and the other signed on with Tarborrow so now I got none."

"I know," Beauford admitted. "There ain't much you can do with things like they are. But I can, and I'm goin' to do it, if my credit is still good at the Mercantile."

Watching him drive on toward town Sheriff Baffert said soberly, "More fuel to keep the fire blazin'."

★ ★ ★

At noon Lee Ransome crossed the upper end of Squaw Canyon where it pinched out against a massive shoulder of the divide. Halting his horse in a muddy seep at the base of a ledge, he watched the roan paw itself a drinkhole in the muck after which the thirsty animal sucked up water noisily.

Ransome was thirsty too, but he hesitated to dismount, not sure he could get back into saddle. Scowlingly, as a man eyeing a deformity he resented but could do nothing about, Ransome contemplated his blood-soaked pants leg. The whole leg was numb now; his left arm was practically useless and he'd lost so much blood that there was no strength in his muscles.

"Weak as a gutted calf," he muttered.

But the water hugely tempted him. He peered down canyon for a long moment and saw no sign of movement among the sun-burnished boulders. He had sighted two riders down there an hour ago, and another up on the rim. A fourth man was probably working the east ridges. Perhaps by now Frenchy Meusette was also in the hunt. That would make five of them. Five guns to one.

When the horse finished drinking Ransome listened intently, keening the windless air for sound of travel. They were waiting for him to make another try at getting through toward town, he suspected, and swore softly, thinking of the attempts that had failed. It couldn't be accomplished in daylight. There were too many of them and they knew the trails too well. But a man could get along without food indefinitely if he had water. So thinking, Ransome dismounted and grunted a curse as sharp splinters of pain lanced his wounded leg. He grasped a stirrup, supporting himself as he knelt in the mud.

The seep water was cool and fresh. Ransome drank, and listened, and drank again. It occurred to him that he had once seen a wounded buck drink in this fear-prodded way, with hounds baying behind it.

Still kneeling in the mud Ransome fashioned a poor cigarette with little help from the numb fingers of his left hand. And because he dreaded the effort of getting back into saddle, he crouched there in the sunlit seep, smoking and listening and wondering if the dull ache in his arm meant that gangrene had set in. A one-armed man would make a sorry homesteader, he reflected grimly. In fact he'd be sorry at most anything, except handling a gun.

Ransome refused to even think about losing the leg. A man would be better off dead. . . .

He knelt there resting, until the faint *clack* of a shod hoof striking stone brought him to his feet. It came from somewhere below; he sent one questing glance down canyon as he grasped the saddlehorn. He said, "Steady, kid — steady," knowing that he would not make it if the horse fiddle-footed now.

The roan stood quiet, making no move as Ransome pulled himself up in the clumsy fashion of a drunken man. Giving the roundabout terrain a brief scrutiny, Ransome rode along a brush-screened trail that climbed northward toward Manana Mesa. . . .

A few minutes later Cameo Kimble halted at the seep and studied its telltale sign, saying, "He got down to drink, stopped long enough to make a cigarette and went up-canyon. We couldn't of missed him by more'n ten minutes at the most."

Society Slim, who had dropped down the east side of the divide, wiped his dusty, sweat-streaked face with a bandana. "He's elusive as an Apache," the ex-cavalryman mused, a hint of admiration in his cultured voice. "Reminds me of the way old Cochise used to give us the slip when the cavalry chased him. It was downright fantastic — most remarkable execution of evasive tactics I've ever seen."

"To hell with Cochise," Kimble muttered impatiently. "High tail up towards the rim. Frenchy should have the line camp boys headed south by now, which means we'll run Ransome into a pocket he can't wiggle out of in daylight."

CHAPTER 9

Dismal Decision

The trail rose steadily, threading its crooked way up the boulder bulged shank of Squaw Canyon, so steep in places that the roan had to claw for footing on slab rock ledges. Ransome halted occasionally to give the sweat-lathered horse a breather and to ease the aching discomfort of his wounded leg. Twice during these brief rests he heard a remote rumor of travel off to the east, and once he glimpsed a sharp gleam of sunlit metal in the brush-tangled canyon below him. That accounted for two riders; but where were the others? The possibility that they might have maneuvered around him and be waiting up there on the divide, nagged his mind with a new worry.

But afterward, when Ransome rimmed out on the crest of a long ridge that fell off into timbered slopes, he loosed a gusty sigh. A man could do a lot of dodging in the kind of country he saw ahead — pine-timbered hills that petered out in a bowl-shaped valley. He scanned the terrain northward, catching the far-off reflection of a windmill's sunlit blades, and wondered if that was Luke Beauford's homestead.

"Could be," he mused, recalling what Kimble had told him about Beauford. And because the hunger grind in his stomach now was worse than the ache of his wounds, Ransome decided to aim for that distant windmill.

He was easing down the slope when he sighted a dust plume rising above a spur of trees to the northwest. At least two riders, he reckoned, and watching the fragile smoke-like banner, understood that they were heading this way. It occurred to him that Kimble might have sent for reinforcements from his line camps, in which case there'd be others coming from the northeast. He shifted his gaze, and presently sighted two riders on a long flat-topped mesa. They also were headed toward the divide.

Ransome swore softly, thinking how high the odds had been stacked against him. Nine or ten to one. Then, understanding that he had escaped the canyon trap Kimble had set for him, Ransome grinned and said, "I'm a fool for luck."

Cameo's strategy had been almost perfect; except for the flaw in timing he would have had his man securely pocketed. . . .

Easing down into timber, Ransome rode at a walk so there'd be no up-swirl of dust to reveal his presence. Those oncoming riders should pass him a mile or two on either side, and unless they happened to cross his trail, they wouldn't know he had slipped through them. Secure in that belief, Ransome relaxed in saddle and let fatigue have its way with him. Fourteen hours of constant vigilance wore a man down; that, and the blood he'd lost and the meals he'd missed made him feel six years older than Satan.

Afternoon's shadows lengthened on the east slopes; they etched mauve patterns across the distant ramparts of Concho Rim while Ransome rode northward with a darkening sense of failure and futility. He had known this deal was loco at the start. But now, because Cameo Kimble had discovered the Lomax note was a fake, it seemed downright senseless. How could a man hope to find a phantom bandit when he had a whole crew of kill-crazy devils hunting him?

"Not a chance," Ransome muttered.

There was only one thing to do now: get out of Concho Basin. He wouldn't leave it with a whole hide, but getting out would be enough. After what Fay Kane's arrival had interrupted last night at Gunman's Camp, just getting out of this country would be sufficient. Tom Rynning wouldn't expect him to buck such odds. He would understand how hopeless it was, now that Kimble knew he was a badge-toter. Tom had said a known Ranger wouldn't stand a chance.

Recalling how he'd said, "You're the one man who might put it over," Ransome frowned. Rynning was wrong about that. All he'd done was come close to getting himself killed. . . .

For a time, slumped deep in saddle and drowsily relaxed, Ransome thought about the homestead he would build down in the San Pedro Valley. He had found a likely spot where the land was too rough to attract settlers who wanted to grow crops along with their cattle. But it would do for cows, which was all he wanted. There'd be no more gunhawking for him — no more fighting and dodging. He would start off with a little jag of good breeder stock. He would brand his own calves and watch them grow to beef steers.

"I'll forget there's such a place as Concho Basin," he mused. Then he thought about Belle Gillum, remembering how the sight of her beside his campfire had revived discarded hungers; had made him woman-conscious for the first time in five long years. The intimate, feminine scent of her hair had strongly stirred him and he thought now: *She's everything a woman should be.*

Rousing himself, Ransome contemplated the country ahead. The windmill, he decided, was farther off than it had seemed. Either that or the roan was dragging its feet. . . .

Once, when intervening timber cut off his view, Ransome thought he must have bypassed Beauford's place. Another time, not knowing he had dozed off, he was forced to stop and study the shadow pattern of surrounding trees before he could orient himself enough to be sure the roan was still traveling northward.

Ransome knew then how thoroughly spent he was — how near physical collapse he had come. It frightened him into a stubborn effort to resist the enervating drowsiness which drugged his senses. He was like that, dazedly clinging to consciousness, when he rode into Luke Beauford's dooryard at dusk.

Vaguely, as though he were in a bedroll with the soogans pulled over his head, Ransome heard Kid Beauford announce, "That's Ransome — the drifter who was lookin' for Gunman's Camp!"

And heard a woman exclaim, "He's been shot!"

Then, as his eyes focused in accommodation to the doorway lamplight, Ransome saw a man move toward him — an unarmed man who said in kindly fashion, "I'll help you down."

He did. His strong hands were gentle as a woman's, his voice quietly reassuring. "Lean on me," he suggested and his body was a stout crutch supporting Ransome when he limped toward the house.

"Don't bring him here!" the woman called sharply. "We've trouble enough without inviting more!"

"I'll need hot water," the man called back, "and some bandages."

For a time none of it seemed quite real to Lee Ransome. He was remotely aware of the woman's complaining voice; something about Cameo Kimble. The man said, "Warm up some supper for him, Ruth. He's had nothing to eat all day."

"That's a fact," Ransome agreed, and

discovered that he was sitting in a chair beside the kitchen table. The lamp-lit room came into focus for him now; a clean, cheerful room with curtains at the windows and the good smell of boiling coffee in it.

A little girl came up to him and said, "My name is Charity. What's yours?"

"Why, that's a pretty name — real pretty," Ransome praised, and seeing how solemn she was, said, "I bet you have dimples when you smile."

But she didn't smile. She just stood there peering at his blood-stained shirt sleeve and saying, "You're shotted."

"Come away, child," Mrs. Beauford called from the stove.

Beauford brought a medical kit to the table and laid out a set of shining surgical tools.

"So you're a doctor," Ransome said, surprised and pleased.

Beauford shook his head. "Started out to be a vet, but changed my mind."

Ransome watched him examine his wounded arm.

"Needs cauterizing," Beauford announced. Then he used his jackknife to cut a slit in the blood-soaked pants leg and prodded the discolored flesh around this ragged wound. "Not deep enough to damage the muscle, but it'll have you limping for a spell."

Kid Beauford came into the kitchen, saying, "Don't hear nobody comin'. How many was chasin' you, Ransome?"

"Five or six, maybe more," Ransome said. "But I don't think they know which direction I took."

"Ezra, you stay out there and listen," Beauford ordered, then turned to his wife and said, "Bring the man a cup of black coffee to give him courage while I work on him."

She did, ignoring Ransome's sincere thanks, and saying to her husband, "I wish you'd hurry, Luke. I surely do."

Ransome sipped the coffee. It was strong and hot, seeming better than any coffee he'd ever tasted.

"We have no whiskey," Beauford said, apologetically. Then he proceeded to cauterize the wounds with a deft sure skill that made the chore mercifully brief; that left Ransome weak and perspiring, and hugely appreciative.

"No medico could've done a better job," he praised. "I'm sure much obliged."

When the bandaging was finished, Mrs. Beauford put his supper before him. "I dislike to hurry a man," she said flatly, "but I wish you'd take no more time eating than is necessary. It might go hard with us if Cameo Kimble should find you here."

"Why Ruth — I'm surprised at you!" Beauford censored. "This is our home and we shall use it as we see fit."

Then he said to Ransome, "Take your time, friend. There is no hurry."

Sheriff Sid Baffert sat in the Circle G kitchen with Big Bart Gillum while Belle washed supper dishes. The lawman had spent several hours endeavoring to untangle a jigsaw puzzle of horse tracks on the east flats without success. "Too much recent travel to tell anything definite," he admitted. "But I still think Tarborrow was tellin' the truth, Bart. I don't believe it was Bootjack that raided you the other night."

"Then who in hell do you think done it?" Gillum demanded scoffingly. "We was raided. Cooky's grave and Kid Beauford's busted arm proves that. So who would of done it, except Tarborrow?"

Baffert puffed on his cigar for a long moment before he said, "Well, it could've been Kimble."

"You're loco, Sid — loco in the head!" Gillum exclaimed in shouting derision.

"Kimble ain't took sides, one way or the other!"

"Perhaps not," Baffert muttered. "But Cameo might be willin' to see Circle G and Bootjack both go busted. He's ambitious, Bart, and slick as cow slobbers. Maybe he saw a chance to stir up fresh trouble between you and Tate, without showin' his hand."

"Your head is full of loco notions," Gillum scoffed.

"Well, what's loco about suspicionin' a man that keeps a crew of gunhawks on his payroll?" Baffert demanded. "I didn't say Kimble done it — but I say he could've. And maybe he did."

Belle turned from the sink, facing Baffert and saying confidently, "Cameo wouldn't raid Circle G. You're wrong about that, Sheriff Sid."

"How come you're so sure?" Baffert asked.

Belle smiled. "Cameo wouldn't permit his men to shoot toward this house," she said.

"Why not? His toughs been usin' Luke Beauford's windmills for target practice, and their bullets struck the front stoop. Why wouldn't Kimble let 'em shoot at this house?"

Belle's lamp-lit face showed a heightened

color, so that now she was like a schoolgirl possessing some secret knowledge that embarrassed her. "He would be afraid a bullet might hit me," she said quietly and went back to washing dishes.

Big Bart chuckled. "Kimble wants to marry her," he explained. "Of course Belle just laughs at him, but he's too much of a romancer to take a chance on her bein' hit by a stray bullet. So it wasn't his crew that shot us up. It was Bootjack, by God, and if Tate Tarborrow said different he lied!"

"Maybe so," Baffert admitted, accepting the logic of that reasoning. He said slyly now, "If Belle should change her mind about Kimble you'd have nine or ten more guns on your side, Bart. Enough to blast Bootjack clean out of the basin."

Gillum didn't like that. A deep frown rutted his massive, weather-honed face and he muttered, "I ain't used professional gunhawks yet, and don't intend to. But I've got to hire some more riders, which is why I'm rushin' this beef drive. I got to have a full crew to keep the Bootjacks in their place."

"I've got a hunch Cameo would be glad to supply some men, under certain circumstances," Baffert mused, as if thinking out loud.

Belle resented that. And she showed it by asking quietly, "Are you still calling on Fay Kane, Sheriff Sid?"

"Yeah," Baffert admitted. It was his turn to be embarrassed now. A ruddy flush stained his cheeks and he said sheepishly, "I guess it's got to be sort of a habit."

Then he asked Gillum, "You startin' your beef drive tomorrow?"

"At daybreak," Big Bart said. "We'll go through the pass on Mormon Ridge and cut across Homestead Valley, which'll save us upwards of fifteen miles. We should reach Beauford's place the second night, and make it into town by dark of the third day."

"I'm going to drive the chuckwagon," Belle announced. "My first trip as camp cook."

Presently, as Baffert went out to saddle his horse and Gillum accompanied him, the sheriff said, "I hope you don't run into no trouble, Bart. Especially with Belle bein' along."

"We'll be ready if it comes," Gillum muttered. "We'll be watchin' for them Bootjack hellions, every inch of the way."

CHAPTER 10

"Run, Goddam You — Run!"

Lee Ransome awoke from deep, dreamless sleep. For a moment, as he peered at thin bright lines of sunlight, he was confused. Then his eyes focused on a knot hole in a warped board and he understood that this was Luke Beauford's barn.

There was a blanket over him and a double thickness of tarp under him, with hay beneath that. "A real soft bed," Ransome mused, and glanced at his horse which stood in hipshot ease at the far corner of this nearly empty hay barn. Someone had brought the roan a bucket of water.

Ransome yawned and got slowly up, grimacing at the multiple aches that movement brought. He felt weak and lightheaded, yet fully rested. He leaned against the wall, favoring his bad leg and thinking of his good fortune in coming to Luke Beauford's home. He couldn't have picked a better place. It seemed downright odd that there should be such a Good Samaritan breed of man in this hate-ravaged country. A man who'd treat a total stranger with such graciousness; who would deliberately ignore the protests of his wife to furnish sanctuary for a bloodstained drifter.

Remembering the bounteous supper he'd eaten last night, Ransome recalled Mrs. Beauford's unrelenting resentment. She hadn't liked it at all. She had kept going to the door and listening, so worried she couldn't sit still. When Luke suggested putting him up in the barn she had said fretfully, "That's liable to get us in trouble with Kimble's toughs — bad trouble!"

Kid Beauford also had seemed to resent his father's kindness to a wounded renegade, but the old man said stubbornly, "Ransome needs a night's rest and he's goin' to git it in my barn. I'll have no more talk about it."

Now, as Ransome limped to the doorway he wondered if Kimble's crew had lost his trail above Squaw Canyon, and guessed they had. A horse wouldn't leave much in the way of tracks on those rock ledges; even a shod horse. Cameo and his men were probably out again today, riding wide circles; but it would take them several hours to cut his sign and follow it here.

Little Charity was in the yard, squatting close to a mother hen with a brood of fluffy chicks. She glanced up at Ransome and said smilingly, "Vivian has eight babies. They came out of eggs."

"They're real nice," Ransome praised. He limped over and hunkered on his heels beside her and added, "So are you."

Ignoring the flattery, she bragged, "Vivian is my very own hen." She picked up a baby chick, holding it gently in dimpled hands and saying, "This is Christine. She's my favorite. Don't you think she's cute like a bug's ear?"

They all looked alike to Ransome. But Charity called each chick by name as she proudly pointed out her peeping playmates. There was Gretchen and Gloria, Annabelle, Evelyn and Judith, Prudence and Mary Jane.

"No roosters?" Ransome asked with mock disappointment.

"Ezra says Annabelle is a rooster, 'cause she's the biggest," Charity reported. "I hope she isn't. Roosters crow at night. They wake you up from sleeping. Like when the bad cowboys shoot at our windmill."

"Yeah," Ransome agreed, "they're sort of a nuisance."

It occurred to him now that men weren't the only ones who had to pay the toll of range war. Women paid it also, in worry and grief; even little girls had to share the burden by having their sleep disrupted.

"I watch my chicks every day, so the bad hawks can't get them," Charity confided. "Hawks have scratchy claws that kill baby chicks."

Then she peered up at Ransome and announced solemnly, "My mommy says you're a gunhawk. Ezra does too."

Lee Ransome had faced that accusation countless times, and regretted it. But never more than now. With Charity's questioning eyes so calmly appraising him, it seemed worse: coming from this sweet-faced little girl it seemed monstrous and indefensible.

"Are you?" Charity prompted.

Ransome nodded, not looking at her — not wanting to see her childish curiosity change to something else.

"Why don't you be like my daddy?" she asked. "He doesn't like guns at all."

"Neither do I," Ransome said.

She looked at his holstered gun, asked, "Then why have you got one?"

Ransome shrugged, having no answer for

her, and now Mrs. Beauford called from the kitchen doorway, "Your breakfast is ready."

There was no friendliness in her voice, nor in Kid Beauford's barely civil greeting. But the scrambled eggs, oven-warmed biscuits and coffee were in generous supply.

Again, as she had last night, Mrs. Beauford kept peering out as if expecting to see riders come from the timbered hills. *She's scared through and through,* Ransome thought and was genuinely sorry for her.

"Did your husband go to town?" he asked.

The woman shook her head. "He's digging post holes on our west line," she said flatly.

Kid Beauford, who'd been sitting on the stoop, came in and asked, "Where you headin' for, now that you ain't welcome at Gunman's Camp?"

"Out of Concho Basin," Ransome said with a self-mocking smile. "That will suit everyone, including me."

It seemed to please the Kid. Some of the sullen dislike faded from his eyes and from his voice as he said, "This is a tough country for strangers. Tol'able tough."

Ransome grinned, and nodded at the

146

Kid's sling-supported arm. "For natives also," he suggested.

Then he thanked Mrs. Beauford for the breakfast and went outside. He was limping toward the barn when he heard the hooftromp of galloping horses to the south. They were somewhere beyond the house, which hid them from view; but he thought at once: *Kimble's crew!*

And at this same moment, as Ransome hurried into the barn, Kid Beauford stood at a rear window, exclaiming, "It's Tanner and Benson!"

He moved quickly toward his gunbelt which hung on a peg near the door; he was reaching for it when his mother commanded, "No, Ezra — don't you touch that gun!"

Charity scurried in to announce breathlessly, "It's the bad cowboys, Mommy!"

Mrs. Beauford pushed Charity behind her as the two riders pulled their horses to a dust-boiling halt before the house.

"Anybody home?" Hack Benson called boomingly.

As Kid Beauford went out of the door his mother warned, "Be careful what you say, son — be purely careful."

Young Ezra halted on the front stoop. "What you want?" he asked, quite sure of the answer, and wondering what to do about it.

"Well, well — look who's here!" Benson exclaimed, winking at Joe Tanner. "It's the Circle G gunslinger in person, by God!"

A mirthless smile creased Tanner's pock-pitted cheeks. "It is for a fact, and lookin' real mean," he said in a thoroughly derisive voice. "Maybe we shouldn't come here, Hack. Him bein' so mean, and all. It's downright hazardous."

"We'll just have to risk it," Benson said. Then he peered at Kid Beauford and announced, "We trailed a feller here named Ransom. When did he show up?"

"Sundown yesterday," Kid Beauford said.

Tanner turned to Benson, demanding, "How in hell could he of got past the line-camp boys?"

"Must of eased past 'em on the divide," Hack muttered. "Never saw the beat of it, the way he snuck out of Squaw Canyon without none of us seein' him. Must be part coyote."

Then he turned again to the Kid demanding, "Which way did Ransome go?"

Kid Beauford shrugged. "I didn't notice," he said sullenly.

"Oh — so that's how it is!" Benson

boomed. "You didn't notice."

And now Tanner warned arrogantly, "Don't try no smart stuff on us, Kid. You give us straight answers or we'll bust this place apart!"

Mrs. Beauford stepped quickly out beside her son. "Ransome said he was leaving Concho Basin," she announced nervously.

"Didn't ask *you*," Tanner snapped, showing no respect for this fear-blanched woman. His squinty eyes remained on Kid Beauford as he inquired sneeringly, "Afraid to wear your nice new gun?"

Hack Benson laughed, said, "He's just a yeller-bellied nester like his old man. Nesters don't tote guns. They ain't got guts enough to fight. He's a counterfeit, just like his plow jockey father."

"Don't you call my father a counterfeit!" Ezra blurted.

"That's what he is, same as you," Tanner scoffed. "All mouth and no guts."

"If my arm wasn't broke I'd show you," the Kid muttered.

"Well, your left arm ain't broke," Tanner said. "Only takes one hand to hold a pistol."

Deliberately, as if proving his point beyond doubt, Tanner drew his gun, transferred it to his left hand and drove a bullet through one of the windmill's revolving blades.

"Nice shootin'," Benson praised, a pleased grin rutting his beefy face. Then he nodded at the nearby chickens and suggested, "Show the Kid how you do with live targets, Joe."

"Don't you dare!" Mrs. Beauford exclaimed.

But Tanner was already firing. His first bullet missed, kicking up dust and frightening Vivian to frenzied clucking. But the second slug struck a baby chick, making it bounce in the air.

As if keeping score at target practice, Hack Benson announced, "One down!"

Kid Beauford whirled toward the doorway, colliding with Charity and pushing her back into the house as the little girl cried, "He shotted Vivian's baby!"

And Mrs. Beauford shrilled, "Ezra — don't you touch that gun!"

Tanner and Benson turned in unison, Hack now drawing his gun. They were like that, squarely facing the house doorway, when Lee Ransome stepped from the barn and called sharply, "Drop those guns — quick!"

It was a queer thing. A brief moment ago these two had been confidently expectant, all their attention focused toward a crippled youngster willing to die for his pride. Now they sat as if frozen in their saddles, bug-eyed with astonishment, thoroughly confused and not knowing which way to look.

"I said drop 'em!" Ransome snarled and drove a bullet through the steepled crown of Joe Tanner's hat.

That did it. Both guns fell to the ground and both faces turned toward Ransome as Kid Beauford came out onto the stoop with a gun in his left hand.

"A fine pair of counterfeits," Ransome muttered, moving across the yard. "Keep them covered, Kid, while I borrow their Winchesters."

Then he holstered his gun.

That pleased Kid Beauford immensely. It made him feel proud. He said, "Sure," and kept a close watch while Ransome pulled the two rifles from saddle scabbards.

Mrs. Beauford sat down on the stoop as if abruptly too weak to stand. Her hands were still tightly clasped across her bosom, but now color returned to her cheeks and she said whisperingly, "Thank God Ezra didn't have to face them alone!"

Unnoticed by the grownups, Charity

hurried to where Vivian was clucking over the dead chicken. Charity peered at her peeping charges, not sure which had been killed until she looked at each one. Then she said, "It's Annabelle," and gazing in wide-eyed wonderment at the mangled thing on the ground, sobbed, "Poor Annabelle."

Lee Ransome put the Winchesters on the stoop, smiled reassuringly at Mrs. Beauford and then ordered his prisoners to dismount.

"What for?" Hack Benson demanded.

"You'll find out," Ransome said, and because they were slow about obeying, drew his gun and commanded sharply, "Get down!"

They dismounted, whereupon Ransome ordered, "Slip off those bridles and hang them on your saddle horns."

"What's the idea of settin' us afoot?" Joe Tanner asked.

Ignoring the question, Ransome took a limping step forward and swung up his gun as if it were a quirt poised for striking. "I owe you bums a pistol-whipping," he warned. "All I need is an excuse — any excuse at all."

That convinced them. They did as he instructed, whereupon Ransome waved his gun and yelled at the horses, spooking them into swift departure.

"Fifteen miles to camp," Joe Tanner muttered.

And Hack Benson cursed viciously.

Ransome turned on the beefy rider, an old sense of outrage in him. He brought the gun barrel against Benson's head with a short slapping motion and snarled, "Show some proper respect for womenfolk!"

Benson teetered back on his heels, momentarily shocked and blank eyed.

Ransome faced Tanner, demanding, "You got something to say?"

The reedy rider moved back a step. His black eyes were bright with an inward heat, but his lips remained tight clamped. He glanced at the gun and shook his head.

"Then start walking," Ransome ordered. "I'm giving you three minutes to hike out of range. After that the Kid and I will do some target shooting."

Hack Benson's thick lips formed a curse, but he thought better of it. Rubbing his bruised head he followed Tanner from the yard without speaking.

Kid Beauford loosed a gusty laugh. "You sure dehorned them rannyhans," he bragged. "You made 'em drop them guns like their fingers was burned."

"No," Ransome disagreed. "It was you and me together, Kid. We had them trapped between us."

Tanner and Benson were out into the road walking fast when Luke Beauford drove his team around the north end of the corral and shouted, "What was that shootin' I heard?"

"Just a little target practice," Ransome reported. He glanced at Charity's dead chicken, that sight rousing a savage anger in him. Drawing his gun he fired a bullet into the road so close to Hack Benson that dust sprayed the big man's boots.

"Run, goddam you!" he shouted. "Run!" And they ran. . . .

At noon a Tarborrow rider sat his horse on a piney ridge and watched the Circle G trail herd move slowly eastward. He built a cigarette and smoked it down while the strung-out cattle plodded through the trees directly below him. A sharp breeze, coming off the west hills, blew hoof-churned dust ahead of the herd, making it difficult for him to estimate their number until the drags had passed.

"Upwards of three hundred head," the Tarborrow rider calculated and grinned, anticipating Tate's pleasure at hearing about this. Discarding his cigarette carelessly he rode along the ridge, keeping abreast of the herd until he had tallied the number of riders. "Five," he said, and presently rimming the divide on his way to Bootjack he observed the Circle G chuckwagon rolling far ahead of the herd.

Had the Tarbarrow rider glanced back at the piney ridge he might have noticed a spiral of smoke rising from pine needles where his horse had stood a few moments ago. But he didn't glance back, and there was too much dust for the Gillum riders to notice a small plume of smoke behind them.

Fanned by a steady breeze, the fire lanced out in a v-shaped arc, racing across tinder-dry pine needles with incredible speed. Bushes flared into brief bonfires; pine cones glowed red and quickly turned to gray ash. A squirrel with foraged food bulging its pouchy cheeks, scampered up the trunk of a big-topped pine and clung there in chattering perplexity while a queer red wave flowed swiftly across the ground. Then, as the strange redness crept up the tree toward him, the squirrel fled to the topmost branches. . . .

Within a matter of minutes crackling flames turned the big-topped pine into a towering torch that exploded with a burst of blazing splinters. Tree after tree took flame until they were like huge pennants — like wind-whipped guidons flapping scarlet tails above billowing plumes of sun-tinted smoke.

Big Bart Gillum, who had raced back to turn a bunch-quitter steer into the herd, was first to smell the drifting taint of smoke. Glancing westward he stared at the flame-ravished ridge and could scarcely believe his eyes.

"Fire!" he blurted, then rose in his stir-rups and yelled, "Forest fire!"

For a moment, as riders peered back in astonishment, the long column of beef steers plodded on without the supervision of flankers or the urging of dust-peppered drag riders. "It ain't more'n a couple miles away!" one rider exclaimed apprehensively.

And another, pointing northward, yelled, "It'll beat us to Sashay Ridge and pinch us off!"

Whereupon Big Bart Gillum bellowed, "Bunch them steers and push 'em hard!"

CHAPTER 11

Warm-Eyed Woman

Lee Ransome led his horse from the barn. He limped over to Luke Beauford who had just buried Charity's dead chicken in the flowerbed. "I'll be riding now," he said and offered his hand. "Much obliged for fixing me up so good last night."

"You're more'n welcome," Beauford said in friendly fashion. He peered at the departing Kimble men who were now far down the road. "Never thought I'd live to see the day them fellers would run off like scairt jackrabbits," he mused. "Not from here. It's a downright miracle."

"No," Ransome disagreed, "just the result of meeting evil with evil — like fighting fire with fire."

Beauford thought about that, his face thoroughly grave. "It's a kind of miracle, regardless," he insisted.

Ransome glanced at Mrs. Beauford who sat on the stoop with Charity and Ezra.

Lowering his voice he said, "I suppose you know that Kimble intends to get this place, eventually."

"I've knowed it for weeks," Beauford muttered, "but I ain't sellin' and I ain't runnin'."

There was no bravado in his voice; no prideful bragging or self-esteem. He spoke in the quiet tone of a meek, yet stubborn man, sustained by the simple courage of his convictions. It was, Ransome thought, a fine thing to hear; and a sad thing, too. For Luke Beauford was doomed. . . .

Shrugging off that futile thought, Ransome climbed into saddle, favoring his right leg. Other men in this country were doomed also, and none of it was his affair. All he had to do now was get out of Concho Basin. One day's ride would put him in the clear, if his luck still held.

"Can I get to Circle G by going through that pass yonder?" he asked.

Beauford nodded. Then, as if struck by a startling thought, he asked, "Say — you wasn't figgerin' to sign on with Gillum was you?"

Ransome shook his head. He saw the interest fade from Beauford's eyes and was wondering about it, when the homesteader said, "If you was wantin' a job I'd offer you one myself."

That announcement astonished Lee Ransome. It seemed scarcely believable that so peace-loving a man would consider hiring a gunhawk. But the surprise of that was trifling compared to what he felt when Mrs. Beauford came over and said urgently, "I wish you'd stay, Mister Ransome. I purely do."

It was an odd thing. This worried, toil-worn woman who had so plainly resented his presence here, wanted him to remain. She was pleading with her eyes. And Kid Beauford was saying now, "Them Kimble toughs wouldn't be so smart-alecky with you ridin' for us."

They were peering up at him, waiting for his answer. Even little Charity, who said solemnly, "You could have one of Vivian's babies for your very own."

A self-mocking smile creased Ransome's gaunt cheeks. He had spent all day yesterday escaping from a trap. But here, he understood, was a different kind of trap, and it was rigged with the most powerful bait of all — a debt of gratitude that needed paying. He shrugged, knowing he wouldn't leave Concho Basin today. Perhaps never. And because he had come so near to taking the easy way out of this deal, Ransome was abruptly ashamed. Luke Beauford wouldn't run from the Gunman's Camp bunch, no matter how much they persecuted him. He just wouldn't run. The kind-hearted homesteader would stay regardless. . . .

"Will you sign on with me?" Luke Beauford asked hopefully.

"No," Ransome said. Then, seeing disappointment cloud Luke's faded eyes, he added, "Not for wages. But I'll use this for sort of a headquarters, if you like."

That puzzled Luke Beauford, until Ransome dug out his Ranger badge and said quietly, "I came to Concho Basin looking for a thief. I quit looking yesterday, but I've decided to give the chore another try. And maybe help Charity scare the hawks away from her chickens in the bargain."

"Arizona Ranger!" Kid Beauford blurted, peering at the badge. "Why, that's what I was plannin' to be!"

Luke Beauford grinned at his wife. "And you called him a shiftless renegade," he chuckled. "You said he wasn't a fit person to have on the premises."

Embarrassment brought color to Ruth Beauford's cheeks. "How was I to know he had a badge hid in his pocket?" she demanded. Then she turned hurriedly away, declaring, "I've got some baking to do."

Luke Beauford was a happy man. "I'll go fix up a good bunk for you in the barn," he announced.

"No, thanks," Ransome objected. "It's just right the way it is and I've got a hunch most of my sleeping will be done out in the brush."

Afterward, with his wounds fresh bandaged and a mid-day meal under his belt, Ransome sat on the back stoop riveting an old saddle scabbard Beauford had loaned him. Looking up from time to time he scanned the southern sweep of the valley. When trouble came it would most likely come from that direction, but Kimble's men might have fanned out far to east or west, in which case they'd swing back and come in from the north. With that possibility in mind, Ransome had asked Kid Beauford to take up his watch on the front porch.

Ransome smiled thinly, thinking about Cameo's reaction to the report Tanner and Benson would eventually deliver. Already smarting from the frustration of yesterday's failure, the boss of Gunman's Camp would be furious. But even so, Kimble might choose to play it safe — might resist the wrathful urge to raid this place now, knowing he'd lose a man or two in such an enterprise.

Cameo's best strategy was to keep his crew intact against the day when a bunch of hardcase riders would be Big Bart Gillum's only chance for survival. Ransome frowned, recalling Kimble's confidence on that score; how he'd said, "She's a trifle choosy, but she'll change when the time comes." Kimble's confidence might be well founded. Belle's loyalty to her father would prompt almost any sacrifice to save him from sure ruin. And it might come to that, if the feud lasted much longer.

Abruptly, and for the first time, Lee Ransome felt a personal interest in the fantastic chore Tom Rynning had fashioned for him. If he could corral the bandit who'd robbed Big Bart — could prove beyond doubt that Jim Tarborrow hadn't done it — the feud would end. And Cameo Kimble's foul scheme to marry Belle would be worthless as a four-card flush!

Ransome grinned, thinking how huge a joke that would be on Cameo, especially if Society Slim proved to be the bandit. . . .

"A loco deal," Ransome muttered, and

remembered saying the same thing the first afternoon on Mormon Ridge. He hadn't known then that he would meet a warm-eyed woman who would give him a dead man's saddle. He smiled, recalling the feminine scent of Belle's hair — how soft and pliant she had been when he pressed against her in the wagon shed, using his body for a shield. No wonder Kimble bragged that there wasn't another woman in Arizona Territory to compare with Belle, and that he proposed to possess her.

Finished with the scabbard, Ransome laid it aside and shaped up a cigarette. There was one far dust head off to the south now; he watched it intently, endeavoring to spot riders against the brush-blotched slope of Manana Mesa. Presently he heard a wagon rumble into the front yard and wondered why Beauford had quit work so early. Couldn't be more than three o'clock. Scarcely seemed that late.

Continuing his squint-eyed appraisal of the far-off slope, Ransome observed a rider quartering northeast. The distance-dwarfed shape seemed to be motionless, but Ransome eyed the risen dust and said, "He's high-tailing toward the road."

That, he guessed, meant the rider had glimpsed Tanner and Benson trudging homeward. He wondered how the embarrassed pair would explain their predicament, when sound of a footstep startled him to instinctive action. Whirling and drawing at the same instant, Ransome came face to face with Belle Gillum.

"My goodness!" she exclaimed, lifting both hands in an involuntary gesture of defense.

Ransome holstered his gun. He said sheepishly, "You startled me, ma'am. Guess I spook easy."

Belle smiled at him. "Your apology is accepted," she assured. She sat on the stoop and nudged back her dust-peppered hat and said, "I'm driving the chuckwagon for Dad. Kid Beauford is filling the water barrel for me."

"Camping nearby?" Ransome inquired.

"Back in the hills about five miles," Belle said. "The herd should reach there about sundown."

Again, as he had the first time he met her, Ransome was strongly aware of the sweet full curve of this woman's lips. They attracted a man's attention, and now, as he sat down beside her, he wondered how it would be to kiss those lips — and was astonished at his rash impulse to find out.

Belle eyed him appraisingly. "So you're

one of Rynning's rangers," she mused.

"On a sort of temporary basis," Ransome explained. "Came here to find the masked bandit who held up your father and then swapped horses with Jim Tarborrow."

Belle laughed, said scoffingly, "What a silly chore."

"Would it also sound silly to you if I said Circle G wasn't raided by Bootjack the other night?" Ransome asked.

"Of course it would," Belle said, "especially if you used Sheriff Baffert's crazy suggestion that it might have been done by Cameo Kimble's renegades."

"Well, Baffert was right," Ransome said and quietly reported what he had seen and heard at Gunman's Camp. "Cameo didn't like it at all, but there wasn't any doubt about who did it."

That news astonished Belle Gillum, and sobered her, so that she asked, "Do you really think there's a chance Jim Tarborrow is innocent?"

Ransome nodded. "I'm sure of it. So sure I intend to find the man who did it."

"And risk your life looking for him," Belle mused.

A cynical smile slanted Ransome's lean cheeks. "I've been lucky up to now," he reflected. "Perhaps my luck will continue."

Belle studied him, understanding that her first impression of Lee Ransome had been correct. He was, she thought now, a man thoroughly conditioned to toughness — a man trained to meet trouble head-on. But he was no renegade with a gun for hire. Even though he possessed a gunman's capacity for fighting, perhaps for outright savagery, there was in him also an inherent gentleness that he could never quite hide. A quality more appealing because he seemed unwilling to reveal it.

She said finally, "If you had been here at the time it happened I'd admit Dad might possibly have mistaken Jim Tarborrow, behind a mask, for you. But there wouldn't be three men so similar."

Something clicked in Ransome's mind. He couldn't identify it, yet an urgent sense of near-understanding caused him to repeat her last sentence to himself: *There wouldn't be three men so similar.* Something about that seemed important; seemed to furnish a clue.

As if thinking aloud, Ransome said slowly, "You told me that first evening that I reminded you of Jim Tarborrow. Now if I also reminded you of someone else —"

Then abruptly the probing fingers of his

mind grasped the elusive clue her words had fashioned: Sheriff Baffert's saying that he looked enough like Cameo Kimble to be his brother!

And Kimble had been in this country at the time Big Bart was robbed. . . .

Swiftly, with the complete absorption of a man assembling intricate parts of a puzzle, Ransome tallied the angles that might involve Kimble. Cameo was tall, the type of scalawag who'd resort to thievery if he needed cash, and smart enough to conceal his identity. But that wasn't enough, Ransome realized; there had to be something distinctly personal — some motive or method that would incriminate Kimble.

"Only one real clue," Ransome muttered.

"What was that?" Belle inquired.

"The bandit wore gloves. Why would a man wear gloves on a hot day?"

Belle said thoughtfully, "Perhaps he wanted to hide his hands. He might've had a scar, or a crippled finger that he didn't want seen."

Recalling Kimble's hands, Ransome shook his head. No scars on those smooth, uncalloused fingers. Then he remembered the matching cameo rings — how Kimble had said he'd won them in his first poker game and *had never taken them off since!*

Ransome smiled, hugely pleased about this. A man could make a capture when he knew who to catch; he could go at it head-on and get the job done. . . .

"You look," Belle suggested, "as if you'd discovered something important."

"I have," Ransome said. He looked at her, and grinned, and now, as she smiled back at him in comradely fashion, a profound realization came to Lee Ransome — a sudden recognition that here was the woman he'd been waiting for, without knowing she existed.

The absolute conviction that this was so, revived every man-want he'd discarded five years ago; it aroused obscure hungers long denied. The intimate scent of her hair; the way her nostrils flared, ever so gently, when she smiled; the womanly richness of voice — everything about her attracted him.

"What did you discover?" Belle inquired, meeting his steady gaze with an equal steadiness.

"You," Ransome said.

"But I thought we were old companions," she objected in mock concern.

Then a mischievous smile formed twin dimples at the corners of her mouth.

It was like a magnet, that smile; an impelling force so powerful and so fundamental that Ransome took her in his arms with the confident ease of a man claiming his own. And her lips were waiting for him. . . .

"Belle," he said huskily, drawing her close and hearing her whisper, "Lee!"

For a timeless interval then, Lee Ransome had no awareness of time or place, past nor future. Nothing before or beyond this moment mattered. There was only the exultant realization that this warm-eyed woman shared the irresistible attraction she held for him — that she was answering the pressure of his embrace with a kindred pressure.

They were like that, with their lips merged in a lingering kiss, when Kid Beauford demanded, "What's going on?"

Belle drew free of Ransome's arms at once. She hastily rearranged a lock of tumbled hair, blushing and not looking at young Ezra.

Ransome met the Kid's bug-eyed stare with grinning assurance. He said censuringly, "You should knock before entering a man's home."

That puzzled Kid Beauford, who said, "But you're outdoors."

"Which is all the home I've got," Ransome explained. "Just the wide open spaces."

Belle smiled at that. "Your house has nice big rooms," she suggested, "and lots of ventilation."

She didn't seem embarrassed now, but the color still warmed her cheeks and there was a glow in her eyes that was like the shine of unshed tears. She looked, Ransome decided, exactly as a woman passionately in love with a Texas drifter should look. The impulse to take her in his arms was so strong that he turned to Kid Beauford and asked pointedly, "Was there something special you wanted to see me about?"

"Not you," the Kid said sullenly. "It was her I wanted to tell somethin' to."

"What was it?" Belle asked graciously, knowing how hugely jealous he must be and feeling sorry for him.

"Well there's a lot of smoke boilin' up over Sashay Ridge. Looks like a whoppin' big forest fire."

"Forest fire?" Belle echoed.

She hurried around to the front yard, and when Ransome limpingly followed her he saw at once that the Kid's prediction was correct. It *was* a big fire — so big that the whole west end of Homestead Valley was blotted out by smoke.

"The herd is over there!" Belle announced in a startled, fear-ridden voice. "Dad will need help with those steers!"

She turned to Kid Beauford, saying urgently, "Please lend me your horse. I've got to go help with the cattle." Lee Ransome, already limping toward the barn, peered at the billowing smoke and thought: *If they're in it now they'll never get out.*

But he kept that grim prediction to himself as he and Belle hurriedly saddled their horses. Instead he asked, "How many men are riding with the herd?"

"Five, including Dad," Belle said. She glanced at him and said in a low, self-accusing voice, "I should've been attending to my business instead of —"

Ransome grinned at her. He said, "The kiss didn't take long, Belle. You shouldn't be regretting it."

"I'm not, really," she admitted, and as they climbed into saddles, said frankly, "I'm glad you're going to be with me, Lee."

CHAPTER 12

Misery Camp

A wild welter of jealousy, disappointment and regret gripped Kid Beauford as he watched Belle ride off at a gallop with Lee Ransome. He had been so stunned by the sight of those two locked in each other's arms that the full significance of what he'd seen hadn't come to him. But it did now, and there was an all-gone feeling inside him; an aching emptiness that was ten times worse than any hunger he had ever known.

It just didn't seem possible that he had seen Belle do that with his own eyes. It wasn't believable that she would let a strange drifter kiss her; not only that — she had hugged him and kissed him back. Kid Beauford couldn't understand it. But Ruth Beauford, who had witnessed the embrace from her kitchen window, understood it well enough. She came out to her son, placing an arm around his shoulders and saying in a pleased voice, "Belle Gillum is a flirt, Ezra, just like I said. She likes to have men handle her and honeyfuss around. She's a born flirt."

"She ain't either," the Kid objected, pulling away.

Mrs. Beauford sighed, and made an open-palmed gesture with flour-dusted hands. "What more proof does a soul need?" she asked. "Proper young ladies don't carry on with almost total strangers like that — especially not in broad daylight. Why you'd of thought they was man and wife honeyfussin' in their own bedroom, instead of in somebody else's dooryard. It was downright scandalous."

Ezra stood in sullen silence for a moment, having no words to refute that accusation. Then, desperately seeking a defense for Belle and wanting to retrieve some fragment of the romantic image she had broken so abruptly, he said, "Maybe it was love at first sight, Ma. Like that story you read to us from *Harper's Weekly*. Maybe they was meant for each other, like them two in the magazine."

That suited Ruth Beauford. "Perhaps so," she agreed. "But in any case she's not the girl for you, Ezra. She's much too old and woman wise for a nice young fellow like you. I'm purely grateful that you've found it out at last."

She peered across the smoke-hazed alfalfa patch and said, "Here comes your pa. He'll be worried for fear that forest fire will cross Sashay Ridge. Do you think it will, son?"

"Hard tellin'," Ezra muttered, not much interested. Then, as he saw how hugely the smoke had spread since first he'd noticed it, he exclaimed, "By grab it might burn the whole blame valley at the rate it's spraddlin' out!"

Other eyes were watching the great cloud of billowing smoke. Tate Tarborrow, leading his crew westward from Bootjack, predicted, "If that fire is where I think it is, them Gillum beef steers will stampede sure as hell."

Anticipation brightened his black eyes and a grin creased his dark, high-beaked face as he added, "In a way I hope they don't."

"Me too," a rider said eagerly. "I'd like to bust that herd same as they busted them three bands of sheep on us."

And some ten miles to the southwest Cameo Kimble sat his horse on a bald ridge with Society Slim and contemplated the increasing smoke haze. . . .

"It looks," Kimble said, "like all the timber in that end of the valley is on fire.

Which means my west line camp gets burned out."

Presently, as they rode northward, Society Slim said, "Wonder how it got started."

"Range has been awful dry for a long time," Kimble muttered. Then he slapped his chaps with an open palm and exclaimed, "Ransome!"

"But why would he do a thing like that?" Society Slim asked in disbelief. "He got away from us, with nothing to keep him from leaving Concho Basin. Why should he deliberately start a forest fire?"

"Revenge," Kimble said, feeling very sure about this.

"Ransome stopped at west camp, filled his belly and then set the shack afire for spite. He probably didn't figure on it spreading like it has, but he's the one who started it, sure as hell. The dirty son has beat us at every turn."

Society Slim nodded agreement. "Ransome operates exactly as old Cochise did. He is using the same tactics — fight, and run, and burn. Elusive as a phantom and smart as a fox. He's a born rebel, that Ransome — an *insurrecto terrifico.*"

"He's a dirty stinking bastard in my book!" Kimble raged. "I should've gut shot him when I had the chance!"

The smoke was an acrid, all-enveloping fog as Ransome and Belle Gillum halted their panting horses on the crest of Sashay Ridge. It shut out the sunlight and turned roundabout country into a weird, unreal region of blurred shapes that loomed grotesquely against a shifting gray background.

Ransome rubbed his smarting eyes and peered westward. "No sign of flames yet," he said, and thought: *No sign of the herd either.* He had loaned Belle his neckerchief to tie across her nose and mouth. Now she lifted it from her lips, saying, "Unless they've changed course they should be directly ahead of us."

They rode down the ridge, keeping close together as their horses moved uncertainly through the smoke-fogged gloom, stumbling over unseen boulders. Crossing a timbered slope and halting again, Ransome heard a remote crackling; and presently he glimpsed upthrust fragments of flame against high-soaring billows of smoke. The fire was close now; dangerously close. . . .

Belle said nervously, "The herd must be this side of the fire. It must be!"

If there's still a herd, Ransome thought grimly. Keeping a big bunch of beef steers together in this smoke-hazed hell would take a miracle of effort. There was no telling which way spooked cow-critters would hightail, once they started running. Nor any way of guessing how far stubborn riders would follow in an effort to turn them back. Once caught in a pocket where the fire had jumped ahead of them they would be doomed to awful death by suffocation even though the flames failed to sear their lungs.

"Where are they?" Belle demanded in fear-prodded impatience.

When Ransome placed a comforting hand on her shoulder, she cried, "Oh, Lee!"

He knew she'd given up hope then, as he had; she was thinking that Big Bart and his valiant crew had been trapped with the cattle they were trying so desperately to save. Yet even now, convinced that further search was futile, Ransome said, "They might've turned south." And understood how flimsy a hope that was, for the fire seemed to be burning in a gigantic crescent that left but one narrow avenue of escape to the east.

When Belle started to ride forward again Ransome restrained her, saying, "We can spot them better from here. Too much smoke and too much racket up ahead."

"Do you think they're done for?" Belle asked.

It was a question Ransome disliked answering. But he met her unblinking eyes directly. "If they're behind the fire they are," he said. "Even though they escaped the flames they'd suffocate."

"How awful," Belle said and Ransome saw that her eyes were brimming with unshed tears.

"I'm sorry," he said, patting her arm again. And at this moment he heard the hoarse, distorted voices of men yelling: "Hi-ya, cattle — hi-ya, hi-ya!"

Belle heard it too for she exclaimed, "Thank God!"

Almost at once then the trail herd came trotting through smoke haze, the big steers closely bunched by four flankers constantly crowding them while one man pushed the drags with a hard swung rope.

Instinctively, without speaking, Ransome and Belle separated, each choosing an opposite side of the oncoming herd. Swinging wide, so as not to spook the leaders, Ransome quartered in from the south and had a brief, smoke-swirled glimpse of Big Bart Gillum who shouted, "Give the drags a hand, friend — we got to hustle out of here!"

Ransome dropped back behind the cattle and joined a shrill-voiced rider he could barely see, so dense was the smoke and dust here. "Boss wants more speed," Ransome reported and began crowding the drags to a faster pace.

"Git on, cattle — git on!"

Gasping, raw-voiced men riding smoke-choked horses. Cursing, rope-swinging men beating the dusty rumps of bewildered, wide-eyed steers; pushing them unmercifully, yet barricading repeated outbreaks that would bring stampede. Pushing, and holding, and cursing. Colliding with unseen windfalls, being hooked by fear-maddened brutes whose broad horns clacked and clattered in the close-packed confusion.

The fire was out-running the herd now, flames racing through timber on both sides. "Faster!" Big Bart shouted hoarsely. "Chouse 'em dammit — chouse 'em!"

A furnace-hot breeze scorched Ransome's back as he spurred his horse against the rumps of running steers. Glancing back he saw red flags of flame envelop a stand of pine they'd just passed through. The fume-tainted air was filled with flying embers now and he thought: *This is going to be close — too goddam close!*

Mile after mile, for what seemed an endless nightmare, while steers sulled and milled; while screeching riders risked their necks to keep fear-crazed cowbrutes from quitting the herd; while half-blind horses collided with smoke-screened trees and crashed through phantom thickets.

"Hi-ya, cattle — hi-ya!"

When a strong gust of wind came off the north ridge the smoke flattened out momentarily like a ground fog. Ransome saw Belle, riding hard on the left flank of the herd and swinging a rope. In the next moment smoke and dust closed in again, but that brief glimpse of Belle whipped up a high-surging admiration in Lee Ransome. It seemed incredible that the woman who'd been so soft and feminine in his arms a couple hours ago could be out here doing a man's work in this heat-scorched hell. What a wife she would make for a Texas drifter who wanted a homestead of his own!

He knew then that the herd would make it. Even though the fire was closer now, he knew Big Bart Gillum's steers would outrun the flames to Sashay Ridge.

And they did. . . .

Luke Beauford rode out to meet the

herd as it came off the east slope. "Plenty of water in my irrigation ditch," he told Big Bart, "and you're welcome to it."

"Much obliged," Gillum acknowledged. "We sure need water."

It was a misery camp they made at dark, with tired-eyed riders remaining in saddle until the last steer had been watered and returned to the smoke-hazed bed-ground a mile west of Beauford's dooryard. Brush fires flamed into brief brilliance atop Sashay Ridge, and northward, where the blaze raged through timbered hills, a crimson glow revealed billowing clouds of smoke against the night sky.

But it was the chuckwagon fire that attracted Lee Ransome's eyes now as he rode toward camp. For Belle was preparing supper, her shadowy, quick-moving shape outlined against the cheerful reflection of glowing coals.

This, Ransome thought happily, might be the last day of the Gillum-Tarborrow feud. Anticipation rose high in him as he contemplated Big Bart's reaction to the news that Jim Tarborrow hadn't robbed him — that Cameo Kimble was the thief who'd held him up. Gillum might not want to believe it, but the evidence would smash down the barriers of doubt, convincing him that he had identified the wrong man. After that there'd be only one thing Gillum could do — make peace with the Tarborrows and thus end Concho Basin's bloody vendetta.

It occurred to Ransome now that he hadn't told Belle. He grinned, recalling what he had told her instead. That would be another piece of surprising news for Big Bart — that he was going to lose his daughter. And real soon. Ransome chuckled, thinking how it would be to ride out of Concho Basin with Belle beside him. To have her for his own. . . .

He was still grinning when he dismounted at the chuckwagon and asked, "Supper ready?"

Belle smiled up at him. "Just about," she said, using a pot hook to drag a Dutch oven off its bed of coals.

Two Circle G riders squatted on their heels, drinking coffee. These fatigue-sodden men peered at Ransome in puzzled fashion and one of them inquired, "When did you join this outfit?"

Ransome tied his horse to a wagon wheel. "Just a visitor," he explained. Glancing at Belle, he added, "An old friend of the family."

Belle smiled at that, and some secret

thought warmed her cheeks with color as she met Ransome's continuing gaze. She said, "Boys, meet Lee Ransome, an Arizona Ranger — Andy Gregg and Lon Peterson."

"Howdy," one of them greeted, and the other said, "Pleased to meet you."

"Same here," Ransome acknowledged, strongly aware of their continuing appraisal. Arizona Rangers, he supposed, weren't overly popular in Concho Basin. . . .

Now Big Bart rode up and dismounted. "We're right on schedule, by God," he said gustily. "Forest fires regardless."

He was like that, a broad grin rutting his massive, smoke-smudged face, when muzzle flare ripped the nearby darkness.

CHAPTER 13

Stampede!

The thudding impact of a bullet against flesh merged with the sharp crack of a gun's explosion. Big Bart's fire-lit frame jerked backward; he loosed a pain-prodded grunt and pressed both hands to his chest as he went down.

All this in the fleeting moment while Belle screamed; while Lee Ransome dropped his saddle and shouted, "Get away from that fire!"

The two Circle G riders scrambled toward the wagon, one of them yelping a high-pitched curse as a bullet knocked him to his knees. A wounded horse reared back on its tie-rope, broke loose and collapsed so close to the fire that its convulsive kicking scattered cooking utensils and hot embers.

Acting on pure impulse Ransome rushed to Belle, picked her up and carried her into the quilted darkness at a limping run.

"Dad is hurt!" she objected. "Let me down!"

"Shut up," Ransome commanded. Ignoring her struggles he swerved away from a loose horse that charged past so close that one outswung stirrup struck Ransome's bad arm. The hurt of it made him wince, but he retained his tight grip on Belle for another hundred feet before putting her down and crouching beside her.

"Nothing you can do now," he said.

"You mean Dad is dead?" she asked, her voice scarcely audible against the yonder tumult of blasting guns.

"No," Ransome said, "but you would be, if you went back there."

The shooting continued steadily. It seemed to increase.

"Those Tarborrow devils!" Belle exclaimed. "They'll butcher the whole crew!"

Ransome cursed softly, thinking how high his hope had been a few moments ago. He'd been so sure Big Bart would believe him, would understand that the feud was a horrible mistake. And that the Tarborrows would understand it also. But there'd been no chance to put his hard-won peace program into operation. . . .

He thought, *Now no one will listen to me.*

Even this woman beside him wouldn't want to hear his talk about Jim Tarborrow's innocence. It wouldn't be important to her after tonight's hellish doings. And now, as Belle relaxed against him, Ransome heard what he had been expecting to hear — the thundering rumble of stampeding cattle, that awesome uproar accompanied by an unceasing rattle of gunfire.

Ransome keened the smoke-tainted air, not sure which way the steers were running. A cold thread of fear crawled through him. Not for himself, but for Belle. The thought of what those pounding hoofs would do to her, turned him sick. It brought him to his feet saying harshly, "Keep close behind me — real close!"

In this fear-prodded moment, as the thunderous rumble increased, Ransome drew his gun. No doubt about it now. The stampede was headed in this direction!

Tate Tarborrow was like a man gone mad. Here, he sensed, was a chance to smash Circle G once and for all. "Kill 'em!" he screeched. "Kill every goddam head!"

The milling herd, surrounded by fast-firing Bootjack riders, made a huge target

— a dark, undulating mass so close-packed that the bodies of bullet-riddled steers were propered upright in the revolving wedge of circling brutes.

"This pays Gillum off for them sheep he shot!" Tarborrow shouted, emptying his gun into the bellowing mass of bewildered steers, and hastily reloading. "Pour it into 'em, boys — chop 'em down!"

Then, as a bunch broke loose beyond him, Tarborrow yelled frantically, "Turn 'em back!" and raced his horse to cut off the escaping targets. Live steers could be retrieved and turned into dollars by Gillum; dollars for buying bullets and hiring riders. But dead steers were buzzard bait and the foul stench of them would mock the man he hated.

"Kill 'em all!" Tarborrow muttered savagely, firing into a shadowy shape that sprawled headlong. "Every last one of 'em!"

But the mill was broken and now a rampaging tide of terror-stricken steers surged eastward in a thunderous tumult of thudding hoofs and clacking horns.

"Hold 'em!" Tarborrow shrilled, firing at the oncoming cattle.

The steady smash of his gun made the leaders swerve, right and left. A steer went down; another stumbled over the carcass and fell, forming a brute barricade against which others piled up. Tate Tarborrow could have outrun the steers, but he remained there in the dust-clotted darkness, firing and reloading, cursing savagely at grunting targets which swerved off on either side.

The stampede was on. Nothing could stop it. But because the main mass of surviving steers had been diverted by one man's lust for slaughter, no more than half a dozen wild-running brutes came close to where Lee Ransome stood with a thoroughly frightened woman behind him — a woman who stood with her arms around him while the muzzle flash of his gun turned the few wild-running steers aside.

"Somebody up ahead did us a real favor," Ransome muttered, hugely thankful.

But Belle's thoughts were on her father, and now, as the last of the steers raced eastward with riders behind them steadily firing, she said, "I must go to Dad, Lee — I must."

"Sure," Ransome agreed, and taking her hand, limped along beside her through dust-swirled darkness.

Almost at once they stumbled against a

trampled steer, Belle falling on the hoof-mangled carcass and shuddering as Ransome helped her up. Off to the left a stricken steer bellowed piteously, and presently, as they reached the spot where Tate Tarborrow had made his slaughter stand, a shoulder-high windrow of dead and wounded animals loomed grotesquely.

"All that beef turned into buzzard bait," Belle said morosely as Ransome guided her around the barricade.

"This will bankrupt Big Bart. It'll break his heart — if he's still alive."

Then, as the chuckwagon's canvas tarp showed dimly ahead, Belle ran forward, crying, "Dad — Dad!"

But there was no answer from the bullet-ravished camp. . . .

Cameo Kimble and Society Slim couldn't understand it. They'd been within sight of Luke Beauford's lamp-lit windows, intending to inquire about Ransome, when the sound of shooting came across the smoke-laced darkness. Their first thought had been that some of their comrades had cornered Ransome, but even as they loped toward the sound of firing, another sound had come to them — the unmistakable hoof-pound of stampeding cattle.

And now, as they eased toward a campfire's ruddy glow on the flats west of Beauford's place, they saw a chuckwagon surrounded by the sprawled shapes of men and horses.

"What the hell?" Kimble muttered.

"It looks," Society Slim suggested, "like old Cochise back on the warpath again."

Then, as Kimble glimpsed Belle Gillum crouched close to a man on the ground, he rode quickly into the circle of firelight and asked, "What happened, honey — what happened?"

"Dad is hurt bad," Belle said, massaging her father's forehead and not looking up. "Andy Gregg is dead, and Lon Peterson is shot in the stomach. I don't know about the others."

Kimble dismounted. He knelt beside Belle, peering at Big Bart's blood-stained shirt and asking, "Has anyone gone to get Doc Smelker?"

Belle shook her head. "No horses, Cameo. Will you go for him?"

"Of course," Kimble said. He patted her shoulder, his voice wholly sympathetic as he added, "I'll drive Doc's rig back myself, honey, to be sure he gets here quick."

Climbing into saddle, Kimble turned to

Society Slim, saying, "Borrow a wagon from Luke Beauford and tote Big Bart over to the house."

"I've already sent for the wagon," Belle said, and now, as her father uttered a deep, choking groan, she cried, "Hurry, Cameo — please hurry!"

Kimble jabbed spurs to his horse. He was riding recklessly southward when he heard a wagon rumble toward the campfire. It didn't occur to Cameo that Lee Ransome might be in that wagon — that he had missed meeting the Texan by a mere matter of minutes. All he thought of now was the hugely satisfying fact that Belle Gillum needed his assistance, that she'd finally asked for a favor. Lady Luck had been booting him around these past few days; the fickle wench had seemed to turn against him for keeps. But she was back in bed with him tonight.

Everything, he thought, was breaking in his favor. The stampede had ruined Gillum's chance to obtain the cash he needed to hire riders. And Big Bart being wounded had caused Belle to ask him for a favor.

Cameo smiled, thinking that Belle wouldn't be so choosy from now on. With her father wounded and most of the crew dead, Circle G couldn't survive against

Bootjack without help.

"Me and my salty crew," Kimble mused and took a thorough satisfaction in the knowledge that his patient planning would pay off. Belle, he reasoned, was woman enough to know what she would have to do. And even though she'd given him no real encouragement, he had sensed a passionate streak in her — a mutual physical attraction that would make it easy for her to marry him. Women were all alike, in his estimation; they all wanted to be taken. Some were harder to get, wanting to be chased before they surrendered. But they all had the same need for a man.

"I've as good as got her," Kimble decided and tantalized himself, thinking how it was going to be on their wedding night.

At about this same moment Luke Beauford tooled his wagon around the campfire and Lee Ransome jumped down, not noticing Society Slim until the tall renegade turned toward him. Then Ransome's fingers closed instinctively around the grips of his gun and he said sharply, "Don't do it!"

Society Slim's right hand had darted toward holster. But now it halted abruptly, as if restrained by some rigid obstruction.

"What are you doing here?" he demanded in astonishment.

"I'm taking your gun," Ransome said, stepping forward.

"But he stayed here to help," Belle objected, "while Cameo went for Doc Smelker."

That announcement startled Ransome. Kimble, he thought now, had lost no time in promoting his scheme to force a frantic woman into marrying him. . . .

"Please put up your gun," Belle said impatiently. "We need this man's help."

"He can help without a gun," Ransome muttered and quickly lifted Slim's weapon from holster. "Isn't that right, *amigo?*"

Society Slim shrugged, saying politely, "My only reason for remaining was to be of assistance to Miss Gillum."

"Then hold the team while Luke administers first aid," Ransome suggested, ignoring the displeasure he saw in Belle's tear-moistened eyes.

Luke Beauford brought his battered veterinary satchel from the wagon. He said to Belle, "This is purely awful, ma'am," and knelt beside Big Bart.

Ransome stood in frowning silence as Belle assisted Beauford with the bandaging. Here, he understood, was the end of any chance there might have been for peace between Circle G and Bootjack. Even though he could prove that Big Bart mistakenly identified Jim Tarborrow, it wouldn't make any difference now. Too much blood had been spilled here tonight. The original reason for the feud would seem unimportant — a trivial thing discarded and forgotten.

Belle, he guessed, understood it also, for he heard her say to Luke Beauford, "There'll be no peace in this country until the last Tarborrow is dead."

A stricken steer's plaintive bellowing drifted across the dark flats and presently Ransome heard the remote howl of a coyote. Those mournful sounds, combined with the smoke-tainted air, were like a symbol — a wild, hate-prodded symbol of this country's doom. And of his own dream of happiness.

Until the last Tarborrow is dead, he thought grimly. Or the last Gillum.

Big Bart mumbled deliriously, "Chouse them cattle — chouse 'em!" His face was ashen in the reflected firelight, but his eyes, wide open now, were feverish with excitement as he exclaimed, "It's them goddam Tarborrows agin!"

"Be quiet, Dad," Belle soothed. "They've

gone, and everything will be all right."

Over by the chuckwagon Lon Peterson cursed in a sing-song chant, and Ransome thought: *Nothing will be right from now on, even if they live.*

He helped lift Gillum and Peterson into the wagon, keeping an eye on Society Slim. Belle got into the wagon and crouched beside her father; she didn't speak to Ransome during the slow ride to the house, nor while he helped transfer the wounded men to beds inside. It was as if he were a total stranger, not worthy of notice; as if whatever had been between them was smothered by an overwhelming need for survival and retribution.

Again the thought came to him that nothing would be as it had once been. But it occurred to him that there was one way the fighting might be stopped. Not by the peaceful meeting between Gillum and Tarborrow that he'd hoped for, and not a very sure way. But it might work, with a little luck. . . .

Herding Society Slim outside, Ransome asked, "Will your horse tote double?"

"I presume so," the ex-cavalryman said, retaining his pose of calm politeness.

"Then we're going to town," Ransome decided, abruptly eager to begin his last gamble for a woman who even now might be watching her father die — who might be the last Gillum left alive in Concho Basin by this time tomorrow.

"What for?" Society Slim asked.

"To see Sheriff Baffert," Ransome muttered, and had his gun cocked when he climbed up behind his prisoner. "I've got a hunch Baffert will be glad to see you, Slim — dead or alive. So don't try anything foolish."

CHAPTER 14

The Fashioning of a Fraud

Sheriff Sid Baffert was playing quarter-limit stud poker in the back room of the Grand Central Saloon when Pat Grogan came in and said, "Cameo Kimble just drove off hell-bent with Doc Smelker, headin' for Luke Beauford's place."

"What's happened now?" Baffert demanded, guessing at once that it concerned Luke's new drift fence.

"The Tarborrows raided Gillum's beef herd," Grogan reported. "According to what Cameo said they shot up the camp and stampeded the steers they didn't slaughter. He said it was the damnedest mess you ever saw."

"Who got shot?" Baffert asked.

"Big Bart and some of the crew. Cameo said Big Bart was alive, but he wasn't sure how many of the rest came out of it. Except Miss Belle. She never got a scratch."

Baffert sighed. He tipped up his hole card and studied it in frowning silence for a moment, then muttered morosely, "An eye for an eye. Raid and raid, in turn."

A miner from the diggings south of town said amusedly, "Them fellers will run out of targets one of these days at the rate they're killin' each other off. There won't be none of them left."

"Which would be a good thing for the country," a hardware drummer proclaimed. He was fifteen dollars loser in this game and so he said impatiently, "Your bet, sheriff."

"I pass," Baffert muttered. A self-mocking grin deepened the lines in his leathery cheeks and he added, "Seems like that's all I know how to do, lately. Just pass."

"Ain't much else a man can do," Grogan sympathized and took Baffert's place in the game. "You heard from that ranger outfit yet?"

"Not a goddam word," Baffert said. Picking up his money he went out to the bar and gulped down his nightcap bourbon.

"Trifle early for bed, ain't it Sid?" the bartender asked.

"Hell, I'm not goin' to bed," Baffert muttered. "I got to do some thinkin' by myself."

"A bad habit to get into," the barkeep warned. "That's what turns sheepherders loco, thinkin' by theirself."

Then he asked, "You mean about the Gillum-Tarborrow trouble, Sid?"

Baffert nodded, whereupon the bartender scoffed, "You'll go loco sure enough if you try to think them rannyhans out of fightin' each other. They'll never quit, Sid — not while there's two of 'em left to trip a trigger at each other."

Baffert nodded agreement and went out, walking in the aimless way of a man having no set destination. Crossing Main Street he stopped in front of the Union Hotel and stood there for a moment. Except for piano music coming from Fay Kane's dancehall, and the barking of a dog over on Residential Avenue, the town was reasonably quiet. But there was no serenity in Sheriff Baffert this night. It made a man feel downright useless, being sheriff at a time like this. It made him feel wore out and draggy, like a gaunt old mossyhorn loafing back in the herd watching young bulls fight.

The piano music reminded him of another thing that increased his dismal sense of futility. There'd been a time, before Cameo Kimble's arrival, when Fay

Kane had considered marrying him. At least she had accepted his courtship in gracious fashion. He hadn't actually asked her, fearing she might consider him too much older. But he'd intended to, and had hoped Fay would accept him, until she fell for Cameo Kimble.

Going on up to the veranda Baffert dropped into a chair and smoked a cigar, taking no comfort from it, nor from his futile thinking. If only there was some way a man could stop the feud while there was something to salvage. Methodically, as a merchant itemizing a list of lost or damaged merchandise, Baffert tallied the names of dead and wounded men — men who had once bellied up to the Grand Central bar, who'd played poker in the backroom, and sat on this veranda of an evening, smoking their after-supper cigars. Good men, most of them, like Harley and Clem Gillum and Sam Tarborrow. Kindly men, like Big Bart had been before he turned sour. And all of them cattlemen. For even though the Tarborrows had turned to sheep as a vengeful gesture after young Jim's conviction, they were cowmen, born and bred. Folks outside Concho Basin probably thought this was a sheep and cattle war, Baffert reflected. But it wasn't, really. There was just one sheep involved — a black sheep who'd turned to highway robbery: Jim Tarborrow.

"Damn him!" Baffert muttered, thinking of all the trouble that young rider's escapade had caused.

There seemed only one way to stop the war: Rynning's rangers. Enough of them to enforce martial law the length and breadth of Concho Basin.

"I'll go down there and talk to Captain Rynning myself," Baffert said, calculating that the round-trip would consume upwards of a week. "I'll take the morning stage."

He was still sitting there on the veranda, considering his plan, when Lee Ransome rode up with Society Slim and asked, "Got a vacant cell at the jail, sheriff?"

That was at eleven o'clock. During the next hour, while he ate a late supper, Lee Ransome revealed his mission in detail to a lawman who listened in astonishment. . . .

"But I asked Rynning for some *Rangers* — not just one," Baffert objected. "If it was a one-man job I'd done it myself. He should have knowed that. What does he think I am — a broke down old cripple that can't hoist his rump off a chair?"

Ransome shrugged, whereupon Sid

demanded, "Why didn't you tell me who you was that first day, instead of actin' like a noose-dodgin' drifter?"

"Well, Captain Rynning wanted me to keep my badge out of it if possible," Ransome explained. "Tom said there'd been a lot of criticism aimed at his outfit lately by the same bunch of politicians that ganged up on Burt Mossman. He didn't want his rangers mixed up officially in a sheep and cattle war if it could be avoided."

Baffert grunted, plainly resentful that the secrecy had included him. "What did Rynning figger you'd do, just by yourself?"

"Stop the feud," Ransome said.

"How?"

"By proving Jim Tarborrow didn't rob Bart Gillum."

Baffert snorted. "By God that's good! I ask for help and Rynning sends me a Hawkshaw searchin' for some way to turn a thief out of prison!"

"He sent me after proof," Ransome corrected quietly.

"How the hell could you git proof?" Baffert demanded. "The scalawag was guilty as a man could be!"

"No," Ransome said, lowering his voice to a confidential tone. "Jim Tarborrow was innocent. You and the jury sent the wrong man to prison."

Baffert laughed at him. He said, "I suppose you could prove that to a court of law," and laughed again.

"I can prove Tarborrow is innocent and that Cameo Kimble is the thief you should've sent to Yuma."

That announcement shocked Sheriff Baffert to silence. He peered at Ransome in wide-eyed wonderment.

"Ten minutes from now we'll go over to the jail office," Ransome continued, "and plant some seed that may give us a harvest in one day's time."

"Harvest?" Baffert asked, eyeing Ransome as if doubting the ranger's sanity. "What kind of harvest?"

Sardonic amusement quirked Ransome's lips. This baffled badge-toter wouldn't know there'd been only one kind of harvest for him since that day in Texas Junction. "A gunhawk harvest," he said softly.

Then, keeping his voice low so the cafe cook would not overhear him, Ransome explained his plan in detail. At first Baffert couldn't see its value, but presently, as Ransome stubbornly proceeded with successive moves and described their significance, the sheriff ceased objecting.

When Ransome was finished he asked,

"How does it strike you now?"

Baffert absently rubbed his chin. He said, "It's a trifle complicated, but it might work."

And then he grinned, adding lustily, "By God I hope it does, friend. I sure hope it does!"

The way he said it, with high hope shining in his eyes, convinced Lee Ransome that he had gained the one thing his plan had lacked — an accomplice for the fashioning of a fraud.

CHAPTER 15

"You're a Gone Goose!"

Society Slim was stretched out on the bunk in his cell, half asleep, when he heard voices in the jail office. Sheriff Baffert, who had seemed reluctant to lock him up in the first place, was arguing with Ransome. . . .

"That's the trouble with you rangers," the lawman accused. "You arrest a man on no charge at all and expect us to keep him in jail until you prove somethin' on him. Well, I ain't runnin' no goddam boardin' house and I ain't holdin' a man on suspicion of bein' a cowboy neither."

There was a long moment of silence now, and Society Slim waited impatiently, wondering why Ransome had arrested him. Cameo, he thought, would be glad to learn that the foxy son wasn't a U.S. marshal after all. For both Tanner and Benson had old scores of train robbing against them.

Finally he heard Ransome say, "I'll lay

my cards on the table, sheriff. It's Kimble I'm really after, but I want to make things easier by taking his crew, one at a time."

"Why you want Kimble?" Baffert demanded.

"For the payroll robbery you sent Jim Tarborrow to prison for," Ransome said.

A hoot of derisive laughter echoed down the jail corridor. "You're loco!" Baffert jeered. "You sound like a sheepherder dreamin' in daylight. Kimble had nothin' to do with that robbery."

"I think different," Ransome said.

There was silence for a moment, then Baffert asked, "What in hell makes you think Kimble had anythin' to do with it?"

Another brief interlude while Society Slim listened intently. This, he reflected, would make a good story for Cameo. . . .

Finally he heard Ransome say, "I've got reasons for suspecting Kimble, but I'm keeping them to myself."

"That's a damn good idea," Baffert said sarcastically. "Don't make yourself look like a half wit by spoutin' half-baked notions about Kimble. He ain't no angel, for a fact, but he ain't no thief. And he's plannin' to marry Belle Gillum if she'll have him."

Then the sheriff asked, "Where you goin'?"

"To the hotel for a night's sleep," Ransome announced, a plain resentment sharpening his voice. "I'm going to watch Gunman's Camp starting tomorrow, until I catch Cameo Kimble — no matter how long it takes."

"You mean you're goin' out there alone?" Baffert demanded.

Society Slim guessed Ransome must have nodded then, for the sheriff exclaimed, "You're loco in the head."

For a time there was no sound save the occasional creak of Baffert's swivel chair. Considering what he'd heard, Slim wondered about the accusation Ransome had made; if Kimble had pulled the Circle G payroll robbery. Red Surdine had known about something that Cameo didn't want told. The ex-cavalryman smiled, thinking now that Red might've known about the holdup and that knowledge had been partly responsible for his death. . . .

Getting off the bunk, he called, "How about it, Sid? What is the charge against me?"

Baffert grunted. He came down the corridor and unlocked the cell gate, asking, "You hear what that fool ranger said?"

Society Slim nodded. "It sounded downright comical, what I heard of it."

"That's the way it struck me," Baffert muttered. He nodded toward the office doorway. "Your gun is on my desk. Ease out of town quiet like, Slim. I ain't holdin' you just to favor a goddam ranger."

"I'm much obliged to you," Society Slim said. "I really am."

And presently, as he rode away from Grogan's Livery, he glimpsed Baffert standing in the jail doorway. The badge-toter, he thought amusedly, might live to regret this night if Cameo *had* pulled the payroll deal. The boss of Gunman's Camp wouldn't want a sheriff to have that information, even if Sid didn't believe it.

Society Slim was a good three miles up the stageroad when Baffert walked to the livery stable wearing a heavy mackinaw and carrying his Spencer carbine. Watching from the livery's lantern-lit doorway, Pat Grogan noticed Baffert's purposeful stride and wondered at the new glint in Sid's faded eyes as he announced, "I'm takin' an important ride, Pat. A real important ride. It might mean the end of the Gillum-Tarborrow fight."

"You mean you're headin' south to git them rangers?" Grogan demanded. "At this time o' night?"

Baffert shook his head. "Goin' north."

"What the hell for?" Grogan asked with an old friend's free inquisitiveness.

Instead of answering that question, Baffert said, "A feller named Ransome will want to rent a horse tomorrow, Pat. Fix him up good. He's a friend of mine."

"Sure," Grogan agreed, watching Baffert cinch up and slide the carbine into his saddle scabbard. "What you up to, Sid?"

"Fixin' for a harvest," Baffert said secretively, and chuckled at the liveryman's bug-eyed stare.

But afterward, as he rode up the steep dugway west of town and thought about the chore ahead of him, Baffert's glowing confidence was cooled by a nagging doubt. There was considerable difference between planting seed and harvesting the crop. A tolerable amount of difference.

Glancing back at the town which now lay far below him, Baffert picked out the second-story lights at the Dixie Dancehall. That would be Fay getting ready for bed. He could picture her in his mind exactly, recalling how lovely her white skin looked beneath the black silk nightgown. Like shadowed ivory. And her lips, so pleasingly red, matching the kimono that was never quite fastened in front. She was a woman to remember, that Fay. A woman to want.

Thinking of what was ahead of him, Baffert wondered if he would see her again. And because he wasn't overly confident, he gave the lamp-lit window a gallant salute.

There was a drumbeat of rain on the hotel's tin roof when Lee Ransome awoke. It slacked off while he was dressing, and had ceased entirely by the time he went down to the dining room where a flirty-eyed waitress greeted him with a sleepy smile.

Wondering about the forest fire in Homestead Valley, Ransome asked, "Been raining long, ma'am?"

"Since around four o'clock," the waitress reported. "Woke me up, and I never got back to sleep."

"Good," Ransome said, thinking that the fire must have been extinguished by so long a rain.

"What's good about me not getting my sleep?" the waitress demanded poutingly.

"Doesn't concern me, one way or the other," Ransome muttered, and wondered if Sheriff Baffert's trip north had been successful. That was the important thing now; the vital connecting link which might make the difference between success and failure this afternoon. And failure would mean death for a badge-toting Texan. There was no doubt on that score; none at all. He would either accomplish the chore today, or die. That was the way the deal was rigged. Tight — tight as a bear trap. The plan wouldn't fail, for the trap would be sprung. It couldn't miss. But because the springing of it involved elements beyond his direct control, there was no sure way of knowing who would be in the trap tonight.

Afterward, as Ransome rode a rented horse up the rain-soaked dugway, he wondered if Big Bart Gillum had lived through the night. That was important also. Belle, he supposed, had not slept at all. She would keep constant vigil at Big Bart's bedside, and be hating Tate Tarborrow more with each passing hour. A dismal sense of loss nagged Ransome as he remembered her quick resentment when he had disarmed Society Slim. Belle's fierce loyalty to her father would include anyone who aided him, regardless of the motives involved; and it would turn her against any man who interfered. Cameo Kimble had recognized this fact long ago, and had patiently fashioned his plan for conquest on the exact pattern of that loyalty.

Ransome frowned, understanding how perfectly last night's raid had rigged the game for Cameo. The boss of Gunman's Camp could be impressively gracious when he chose. He had probably never been less than gentlemanly in front of Belle. It occurred to Ransome now that he had never heard the Gillums say anything against Kimble. All their disdain had been directed at the renegade crew Cameo employed. The man was clever. He made no bones about his crew, nor bothered to apologize for them. If Belle had asked him why he hired such men he probably had told her frankly that he wanted a rough, tough crew that would make him independent of either Circle G or Bootjack. And he would have made it sound reasonable.

"A smooth rascal," Ransome mused. Smooth enough to keep Fay Kane at his beck and call, even though she knew he was courting another woman. . . .

Because the time element was in his favor today, Ransome rode at a leisurely pace. Society Slim, he felt sure, had delivered the news to Kimble at Beauford's place hours ago. Cameo should be at Gunman's Camp by now, making preparations to receive a welcome guest. Ransome wondered how many men Kimble would leave at Beauford's to guard the Gillums against further raiding by Bootjack. The four line-camp men, Ransome reckoned, which meant Cameo would have Society Slim, Hack Benson and Joe Tanner with him.

Ransome thought cynically: *A regular reunion of old acquaintances,* and could easily imagine how glad they'd be to see him; how eagerly Kimble would welcome him back. The man must be fairly seething with anticipation right now.

The sun came out shortly before noon, its welcome warmth banishing long streamers of mist from washes and arroyos. By the time Ransome started up the steep trail to Rimrock Reef the clouds had merged into one long high bank of fleecy whiteness above Concho Rim. Rain water had washed out all sign of travel on the trail, but afterward, as Ransome scouted the Reef's slab rock crest, he saw several cigarette butts, one so recently discarded that it was still burning.

A lookout, Ransome thought at once. Dismounting with proper regard for his bandaged leg, he escorted his horse across the summit to where a rock upthrust formed a shoulder-high barricade. Here he halted, giving Gunman's Camp a questing appraisal. There were no horses in the corral, nor any saddles on the kak pole. Ransome watched the yard for upwards of five minutes, seeing no sign of life. The place appeared to be deserted, as he had expected; it was an open invitation to trouble.

Shifting his gaze, Ransome peered toward Homestead Valley. There was no trace of smoke — nothing to indicate the holocaust of raging flames and blasting guns which had turned it into a hell of death and destruction yesterday. He gave the timbered terrain northeast a thorough scrutiny and was disappointed in its lack of sign. Then the thought came to him that there would be no telltale dust to reveal travel on the back trails today, because of last night's rain. A dozen men, screened by brush or timber, could be on the move without a watcher spotting them from a distance.

Acting on pure impulse, Ransome went back across the crest. He squatted on his heels beside a huge boulder, shaped up a cigarette and had it half smoked when he observed movement in the brush below — a single rider easing along a rocky ledge and sliding his horse into the trail. That, Ransome supposed, was Kimble's way of making sure that his expected guest would not turn back once he'd topped Rimrock Reef.

"Playing it dead sure, as always," Ransome mused.

He finished his cigarette, waiting until he identified the rider as Society Slim. Then he limped back to his horse, and climbing clumsily into saddle, rode eastward along Rimrock Reef. This deal had shaped up exactly as he'd anticipated: the horseless corral, the lack of life anywhere around the camp, and the discarded cigarette butts had been expected. He hadn't foreseen the presence of a rider south of the Reef, but even that fitted the general frame perfectly. Now, if there was a way to descend northward without using the chute trail. . . .

There was. A steep, narrow slide that dropped off into a great heap of loose shale some three miles east of Gunman's Camp. Riding due north through timber Ransome watched the rain-soaked ground for sign. After a mile of this he quartered westward and scrutinized the ground with frowning impatience until he halted to peer at fresh horse tracks that were headed south. Two riders, he decided, going at a slow walk.

Ransome grinned, and crossing the trail,

rode for fifteen or twenty minutes before turning southward. The sun was low now, not penetrating the high stand of timber. It was cool here in the pines, with wetness still clinging to the underbrush. And now, because he was nearing Gunman's Camp, a deeper coldness seeped into Lee Ransome — the gambler chill of a man risking his last blue chip.

Remembering what he had told Sheriff Baffert last night, Ransome smiled thinly. He had called it a harvest, but it might turn into a famine, unless Lady Luck had her arm around him. It occurred to him now that there was still time to change his mind; that he could ride out of here without much risk, even yet. But he shrugged that thought aside. A man couldn't run away from himself, no matter how far he rode. He could never banish the memory of a warm-eyed woman who was fiercely loyal to her father, nor a peace-loving homesteader who said grimly: "I ain't sellin' and I ain't runnin'." No matter how far he rode a man wouldn't forget a dimpled little tyke in pigtails sobbing over a dead chicken named Annabelle.

No, he couldn't turn back. Not when there was a chance to save those people from further heartbreak. A good chance,

Ransome reflected; and it was like a cheerful flame that warmed him as he rode through the dusk-veiled timber. For the first time in his gunsmoke career he was not motivated by hate — by a selfish need for retribution. For even though he despised Cameo Kimble there was no hatred in him. The success of this desperate deal would win him nothing beyond the satisfaction of completing a difficult assignment and repaying a few gracious favors. But it would win plenty for Luke Beauford, and although she might not realize it, for Belle Gillum also.

He thought: *The feud may be finished by this time tomorrow,* and that realization fanned the cheerful flame inside him. He was passing a windfall just north of the yard when Cameo Kimble called sharply, "You're a gone goose, lawdog!"

CHAPTER 16

Dread of Death

Lee Ransome halted at once, neither turning his head nor moving his right hand. This was the moment he had dreaded — the heartbeat of time when the difference between living and dying depended on the unpredictable whim of a man who could kill him cold-turkey. A man itching with the desire to kill him. . . .

In this interval of awful expectancy Ransome played the only card left in the deck for him: he appealed to Kimble's vanity, asking, "How'd you know I'd be here, Cameo?"

Kimble chuckled. "You'd be surprised at what I know," he bragged. Then he shouted, "I've got him, boys — right on the end of my gun!"

A secret sigh of relief slipped from Ransome's lips. The moment he had feared most was over — the first and biggest gamble of all was won. For he was still alive. The rest of it might be bad. God-awful bad. But now there was a chance.

Hack Benson galloped in from the west. He pulled up close and snatched Ransome's gun from holster and blurted, "By God I'm glad to see you!"

Ransome sensed instantly what was coming. He tried to dodge the down-slashing gun barrel. But he was too late. It struck him a glancing blow on the right temple, momentarily stunning him so that he slumped forward in saddle.

Vaguely, as from far off, he heard Kimble protest, "Don't spoil the fun, Hack. Give him a chance to wake up."

They were on both sides of him now, supporting him as the horse moved forward. When they rode into the yard Joe Tanner came up and said complainingly, "You should of made him walk barefoot, to pay for them blisters I got hoofin' it all the way from Beauford's place."

"He'll have blisters aplenty before we finish with him," Hack promised. "More goddam blisters than you ever saw."

Kimble ordered, "Go bring Slim in while we escort our guest into the house."

Still groggy from the pistol-whipping, Ransome dismounted. Blood dribbled down the right side of his face; he wiped it away as he limped to the kitchen stoop where Frenchy Meusette stood framed in the doorway's shaft of lamplight.

"Fix Mister Ransome a cup of nice strong coffee," Kimble told Meusette. "The poor unfortunate fellow has a headache."

Ransome followed Frenchy into the kitchen, took a chair at the table and gingerly explored the gash on his temple. That was one thing he had overlooked in his planning last night — Hack Benson's lust for personal revenge.

Kimble took a chair across the table. His lean face was freshly shaved, creased now by a smile that brightened his milky eyes. He looked, Ransome thought, like a man thoroughly pleased with himself and with all he beheld. . . .

"You didn't suspect that Slim would get out of jail last night and tip me off to your plans, did you, Ranger," he chuckled.

Ransome peered at him as if not understanding what he meant. "You mean Baffert turned Society Slim loose?"

"Sure," Kimble said, "which is why we had the welcome committee all set for your arrival. If it hadn't been for Slim there'd of been nobody here but Frenchy. And he ain't much company, all by himself."

Meusette placed a cup of coffee in front of Ransome. Joe Tanner came into the kitchen followed by Society Slim. The ex-cavalryman peered at Ransome's blood-stained face and asked with exaggerated concern, "Did you meet with a mishap, Ranger?"

"He met with the muzzle of my gun," Hack Benson announced. "Just like he done to me."

"You boys better go feed the horses," Kimble suggested. "We'll be riding after supper."

"How about him?" Joe Tanner inquired, nodding at Ransome.

"He'll take a little ride also," Cameo said smilingly. "But not very far."

The crew went out, and Kimble mused, "So you finally figured it out."

"What?" Ransome asked, revealing slight interest.

"Why the bandit wore gloves on a warm day."

Frenchy Meusette was preparing supper now and the appetizing odor of frying beef filled the kitchen. Recalling the last meal he'd eaten here and what had taken place afterward, Ransome took a secret satisfaction in the comparison. He had been as near death that night as a man could be, with only the fragile hope of survival to sustain him. But tonight was different; so hugely different that he could scarcely keep from smiling.

"You hear what I said," Cameo asked impatiently.

"Yeah," Ransome muttered. "About the gloves. I still don't see why you didn't take off the rings, instead of hiding them with gloves."

Kimble shrugged. "I'm a trifle superstitious," he admitted. "That's why you're going to get a good supper before you go yonderly."

"That's real nice of you," Ransome said, wanting to keep the talk going. "Things worked out just right, didn't they, Cameo?"

Kimble laughed, hugely enjoying this. "I made 'em work the way I wanted," he bragged. "Remember what I told you that first day? How I had things all planned out. Well, beginning tomorrow, I'm the big boss in this country — and I'll have the prettiest wife in all Arizona Territory."

"Belle Gillum?" Ransome asked disbelievingly.

Kimble nodded. "Belle has promised to marry me the day I bust Bootjack. And that won't take long, considering that Tarborrow won't be expecting a fight when

222

me and the boys ride into his place tomorrow evening. We might even catch 'em at the breakfast table, which would make it real simple."

"You mean you're going out to cut 'em down without a chance?" Ransome asked.

Cameo giggled. "How the hell else would you expect? A man can't fuss with fancy scruples when he's out to win himself a whole goddam cow country. And a sweet-loving woman in the bargain. Tate Tarborrow ain't nothin' to me, one way or the other. He's just a galoot with a warrior outfit that needs bustin' and I happen to have the crew to do it. There won't be no witnesses. They'll all be dead, includin' Sam Tarborrow's wife."

Even though Ransome had expected the grisly admission, and hoped for it, the monstrousness of it — the almost jovial declaration that unsuspecting men would be butchered in cold blood — sickened him. And this was the man Belle had promised to marry.

"It'll be easy as blowing out candles on a birthday cake," Kimble bragged.

Or killing a little girl's pet chicken, Ransome reflected.

Then, as if thinking aloud, he said slowly and distinctly, "You started all the trouble by robbing Bart Gillum and putting the blame on young Tarborrow. Now you're going to finish it by wiping out Bootjack."

"Exactly," Cameo agreed, a self-satisfied smile creasing his lamp-lit face. "They'll be calling me Cattle King Kimble a year from now. I'll be the brass-riveted boss of Concho Basin. If things go the way I plan there'll be Heart K line camps all over this end of Arizona in five years' time."

Lee Ransome smiled. He sat back in his chair, thoroughly relaxed and thought: *There it is!*

The crew came trooping in to supper, their spurs setting up a musical jingle. Ransome gave the rear window a surreptitious glance, saw a flimsy streamer of skillet smoke slip through the opening in a graceful, swan-like glide. This deal, he thought, had shaped up perfectly; even better than he'd dared hope. So far. If those horse tracks he had seen this afternoon meant what he believed they did, there was no reason why the rest of it shouldn't go equally as well.

"Eat hearty," Kimble invited. He was the personification of graciousness now. A happy, generous host. Good humor fairly dribbled from his voice as he said, "I feed my guests well. Even if they happen to be Arizona Rangers."

The three riders were seated now and Joe Tanner asked, "You goin' to let me pay him off for them blisters, Cameo?"

"Well, we won't have much time for funning," Kimble said evasively. "I promised Miss Gillum I'd be back this evening to keep her company." He winked, adding slyly, "A man shouldn't keep his bride-to-be waiting around when she's hankering for his hugs and kisses. Not when she's a growed woman and full of fire."

Ransome thought: *You stinking parlor house sport!*

"It won't take no time at all," Tanner promised. "Just long enough to pull off his boots, tie his hands behind him and slip a loop over his head. He'll sprout a crop of blisters before we've went a mile."

Hack Benson chuckled, saying, "If your horse should bust into a run the Ranger would be just one big blister."

"That's no fit topic of conversation at a supper table," Society Slim objected. "In fact it's downright revolting."

Hack Benson laughed, asked, "Would you rather we'd talk about women, Slim — that swivel-rumped one that Red liked so well?"

"A slut," Society Slim muttered disdainfully.

Which was when Ransome saw Sheriff Baffert step through the doorway with a gun in his hand, and heard Tate Tarborrow call from the rear window, "Sit still, you stinkin' sons — sit awful still!"

The fork in Cameo Kimble's fingers remained poised an inch from his slack-jawed mouth. He stared at Sheriff Baffert in wide-eyed astonishment, but it was Tate Tarborrow's voice that held him rigidly motionless — that drove a thrusting dread of death sharply through him.

"So you flimflammed my boy into prison!" Tarborrow taunted in a rage-clotted voice. "And you figgered to chop me down in my own house!"

Then an overwhelming wrath got the best of him and he shouted, "Grab for your gun, Kimble — grab for it!"

No man ever sat more motionless than Cameo Kimble now. Not a muscle moved. Not so much as an eyelid. He was like a wooden man. Like a carved statue. . . .

"Go easy, Tate," Baffert counseled, keeping the table covered with his gun. He grinned at Ransome, saying, "You took a tol'able chance, friend, lettin' yourself be ketched by this bunch of hydrophobia skunks. I knowed they was bad, but by God I never thought they was mad dogs."

Then he added gustily, "The seed we planted turned into a gunhawk harvest, just like you figured it would. Now all we got to do is dehorn 'em."

That didn't make sense to Kimble. What seed was Baffert talking about. He lowered his fork slowly, watching Ransome take Hack Benson's gun from holster and saw Hack dodge as the Ranger drew it up as if to strike. Then, as Ransome disarmed Society Slim he said to the ex-cavalryman, "You toted the seed real good, *amigo*."

Kimble understood then why Sid Baffert had released a prisoner last night. . . .

The knowledge that he had been deliberately framed into revealing himself before witnesses spawned an intolerable sense of frustration that was akin to self pity. It didn't occur to Kimble that all his grown years had been spent in shifty maneuvering and tinhorn trickery. There wasn't the slightest remembrance of gullible men ruined by marked cards or the trusting women he had debauched. All he thought of now was that he, Cameo Kimble, had been hugely, horribly tricked.

"Framed!" he muttered, mouthing the word in a growling disgust. "Framed by a goddam Arizona Ranger!"

He had won so many gambles that winning had become a habit. To lose this, the biggest gamble of all, seemed a monstrous reversal. An unbelievable, fantastic thing. And at this moment, with the awful need to win clawing at his senses Kimble became aware of Frenchy Meusette's brooding eyes. The little cook stood against the side wall near the stove. He shifted his glance toward the bracket lamp, then peered questioningly at Kimble.

Cameo understood instantly what Meusette meant to do. Understood also that the little cook would die doing it. But Frenchy's death wasn't important. Nothing was important now except getting out of this room alive and free. Because there might be that chance for survival in the thing Frenchy was willing to do, Kimble nodded his head.

CHAPTER 17

Red Reaping

Lee Ransome had slipped Benson's gun into his own holster. Now, as Tarborrow eased through the doorway and took up a stand beside Sheriff Baffert, Ransome laid Society Slim's weapon on the table. He was moving around to get at Joe Tanner when Baffert said amusedly, "They're keepin' tol'able quiet, for gabby galoots. Must be they got it all said."

Ransome grinned. This deal was just about over, and because he had two witnesses, Belle Gillum would have to believe the truth of Kimble's treachery. Cameo's confession might sound a trifle fantastic, but she would believe Sid Baffert. . . .

Joe Tanner's pock-pitted face showed a tight-lipped scowl. There was a metallic shine in his lamp-lit eyes, and now Ransome noticed a queer thing: the reedy gunhawk wasn't looking at him, nor at the two men near the doorway. He was peering intently at Cameo Kimble.

Ransome glanced at Kimble, saw his lips pucker into a whistling pout and at this same instant Sheriff Baffert yelled, "Git back, Frenchy — git back!"

The room-trapped roar of Baffert's gun merged with Meusette's shrill dog-like whimper and the crash of a shattered lamp chimney. The table heaved upward, knocking Ransome off balance. He collided with a chair and fell headlong as muzzle flare slashed the darkness on both sides of him.

For a stunned moment he couldn't believe it. Couldn't believe that this thing was happening. It had come with such abruptness that it didn't seem real. Yet the smash of those guns was real and so was the air-lash of bullets. . . .

Swiveling around, Ransome reached out with his gun, feeling for the capsized table, then recoiled as boots tromped his bad leg. This man fired, the gun so close that Ransome felt the heat of its explosion and glimpsed Joe Tanner's fiercely scowling face above him. Ransome fired twice, driving two bullets up at Tanner and then cursing as the renegade fell on him. Tanner coughed once, spewing blood into Ransome's face. Ransome pushed him off, sensing that he was dead, and heard Hack Benson yell, "I got no gun —" that frantic bellow ending in an agonized screech.

Ransome glimpsed a shadowy shape briefly outlined against the window's square of pale moonlight. He emptied his gun at the vague target, not sure he had hit it, and was hastily reloading when Tarborrow called from over by the doorway, "Is that you, Ranger?"

"Yeah," Ransome said and moved quickly aside, expecting a shot. But there was none, and he asked, "Where's Baffert?"

"Dead, I guess," Tarborrow muttered. "He never even grunted."

Ransome swore softly. It seemed incredible that Frenchy Meusette's smashing of a lamp should have upset things so completely; that one man's suicidal action had turned this room into a bloody shambles.

Transferring his gun, Ransome took out a match, thumbed it to flame and flipped it across the room. In that brief flare he glimpsed four bodies, one of them draped across the window sill. Quickly lighting another match he held it long enough to identify the four — to understand that Kimble was missing!

Tarborrow had also lit a match; he

peered down at Baffert and announced, "Shot through the head."

Then he asked, "How about Kimble?"

"He got out the window," Ransome muttered, feeling his way around the table.

Tarborrow loosed a snarling curse. "I got to get that bastard," he exclaimed. "I got to git him!"

And in the next moment, as he rushed out to the stoop, Tarborrow yelled, "You ain't goin' no place, Kimble!"

Two guns exploded in unison, and one of them kept on blasting. Ransome ran through the doorway, narrowly avoiding collision with Tate Tarborrow who was down on his knees and gasping for breath. Then he saw Kimble. . . .

Cameo was in saddle, turning his horse away from the corral hitchrack. Moonlight slanted sharply from the gun in his hand and now, as Ransome stepped around Tarborrow's sprawled shape, that gun exploded.

The bullet tore through Ransome's right sleeve, the tug of it making him miss his first shot. But he didn't miss the second. Kimble yelped a curse and lurched sideways, and fired again, that slug going wild as his frightened horse shied off.

Ransome took deliberate aim. He muttered, "This one is for Baffert," and drove another slug into that swaying, moonlit shape.

Kimble slumped forward, momentarily balanced across the withers of his horse. Then he fell headlong as the excited animal lunged into a run. Kimble's body twisted as it struck the ground, his left boot hung in the stirrup and now the horse raced out of the yard in frantic flight, endeavoring to outrun the dragging thing that bounced along the rocky ground. The limp and mangled and disintegrating thing that would not cease its grotesque bouncing.

Half sick to his stomach, Ransome turned to look at Tate Tarborrow who sprawled unmoving on the moonlit stoop. Blood dribbled from one corner of Tarborrow's slack-jawed mouth. The blank, unblinking stare of death was in his eyes.

Ransome shivered. He felt old, and cold, and worn out. A sense of awful aloneness was in him as he limped across the yard; aloneness and unreality. Even the livery horse seemed to share the feeling of abandonment for it whinnied softly as he untied the reins and climbed into saddle. There was a stillness in the yard that was like the hush of death, so strict that the slight creak of saddle leather sounded loud.

When Ransome rode past the cabin he cursed, thinking of what was in there. This was the harvest Sid Baffert had joked about. A gunhawk harvest. It had ended the Gillum-Tarborrow feud, but not in the way intended. And because he was the lone survivor, Ransome understood that there'd be no use telling Belle about it. No use at all.

It was a dismal ride. Even though he had accomplished the chore Tom Rynning had sent him here to do, Ransome took no satisfaction in it. Frenchy Meusette had seen to that. . . .

"Damn him to hell," Ransome muttered.

And remembering how Kimble had looked being dragged to death, he felt sick again.

Pat Grogan was taking his ease in the livery stable's lantern-lit doorway when Ransome rode in and dismounted. "How much I owe you for the horse?" Ransome asked wearily.

"Well, bein' as you're a friend of Sid's and he's a friend of mine, it'll be just one silver dollar," Grogan said. "Where's Sheriff Sid?"

"At Gunman's Camp," Ransome announced frowningly. "You better take a wagon out there and get him."

"You mean he's hurt?"

"Dead," Ransome muttered.

"God A'mighty!" Grogan croaked. "What happened?"

"A shootout," Ransome said. "You'll need some help. There's six bodies at Gunman's Camp, and what's left of Cameo Kimble is somewhere out in the brush."

That news shocked Grogan so that he just stood there with his mouth open as Ransome turned and walked away. Then he hurriedly followed, demanding, "You mean seven men got killed out there tonight."

Ransome nodded, said, "Baffert, Tarborrow, Kimble, Tanner, Benson, Society Slim and Meusette."

"Lordy, Lordy," Grogan said. "Seven men killed all to once. How many was in the fight?"

"Just them, and me."

"Luck of the Irish," Grogan mused. "You must be the luckiest man alive."

Ransome asked, "When is the next stage south?"

"One o'clock tomorrow afternoon," Grogan said. "You leavin' on it?"

Ransome nodded. "I'm not only leaving. I'm forgetting there ever was a hell-hole called Concho Basin."

He limped on along the moonlit sidewalk in the slow fashion of a man not quite drunk and not quite sober. He thought: *I need a drink,* but when he came to Ringo Alley he remembered Fay Kane and knew there was one more chore that needed doing. A chore he dreaded. . . .

She stood on a stool, putting out the last high bracket lamp, when Ransome stepped into the deserted dancehall. "Closed for the night," she announced, not turning to look at him.

Then, as he just stood there, she glanced over her shoulder and exclaimed, "Why, Lee — what are you doing here?"

Ransome said morosely, "I've got some bad news," and saw the swift change of her expression.

"About Cameo?" she asked.

Ransome nodded.

"Is he hurt bad?"

"He's dead."

Fay Kane peered down at him, her lowered lashes making sooty shadows against her cheeks. "Dead?" she whispered, and absently fingered a cameo brooch that adorned the low-cut front of her green gown. "Cameo dead?"

Ransome nodded, guessing that Kimble

had given her that brooch with the same careless gallantry that he'd given her his kisses. A poor substitute for a wedding ring. . . .

Fay blew out the lamp. She came over to Ransome and took his arm and said, "Come upstairs, Lee. We'll have a cup of coffee while you tell me about it."

"Not much to tell," Ransome said, wanting to get away. "Except that I shot him."

But she kept hold of his arm, guiding him up a dark stairway and into her living quarters. "You look all fagged out," she said, pushing him into a chair at the kitchen table. "The coffee will be done in a jiffy."

Ransome couldn't understand it. She hadn't shown the slightest sign of resentment, and did not now. Yet he had told her that he killed Cameo. He had expected a tirade of shouted abuse, or hysterical grief — anything but this. It was beyond understanding.

As if she sensed his bewilderment, Fay said, "I knew he'd get it, sooner or later. It was in the cards." Then, as she poured the coffee, she added quietly, "And I knew he would never marry me."

She looked at him from across the table, her eyes steady and honest and undisturbed by false pride. "You see," she explained, "I've been around long enough to know how it is with men like Cameo. They want every pretty woman they see. Especially the ones that are hard to get. Cameo got me easy. He took what I gave him and called me his girl. But Belle Gillum was the one he really wanted — the one he had to have, even if it meant marrying her."

She was, Ransome thought, more honest than most of the respectable women who looked down their noses at a dancehall proprietor. And a lot nicer to look at.

Fay came around the table, glanced at the soiled bandage on his arm, and said, "I'll change it for you, Lee, while you tell what happened."

He did, giving himself none the best of it. "I'd forgot about Frenchy Meusette being Kimble's tail-wagging dog. That carelessness cost the lives of Sid Baffert and Tate Tarborrow."

"Oh, my God — is Sid dead?"

That surprised Ransome. Why, he wondered, should Baffert's death mean so much to her.

Again, as she had before, Fay seemed to read his thoughts for she said, "Poor Sid was in love with me. He said I was the only woman he'd ever really wanted to marry. Even when I took up with Cameo, Sid kept coming to have coffee with me in the morning. There was some thing awful nice about him, Lee — something sort of noble. Like a good horse."

"Yeah," Ransome agreed. Then he mused cynically, "So my carelessness cost you two lovers, instead of one."

"Not your fault," Fay murmured, tying the fresh bandage.

Presently, as Ransome got up to go, he said, "Well, I guess you're sole owner of the Heart K outfit now, aren't you, Fay?"

She nodded. She looked at him thoughtfully, adding, "I'll need a man to run it on a fifty-fifty basis."

She was standing close to him now, and there was a warmth in her eyes as she murmured, "A tall, hungry-looking man just about your size, Lee — if you'd like the partnership."

The utter irony of it struck Ransome with an impact that made him loose a hoot of laughter. Cameo Kimble, who'd died wanting Belle Gillum any way he could get her, had lived long enough to ruin another man's chances. Now the other man was being offered a half share in Gunman's Camp. It was a fitting finale to a thoroughly loco deal, he supposed.

"What's so comical?" Fay asked. "Is there anything odd about a woman offering a man half interest in her ranch?"

Ransome shook his head. "It just struck me funny, is all."

"Why should it?" she demanded. "You knew I liked you, way back in Texas Junction. And you knew it the other night at Gunman's Camp. It's been that way ever since you saved me from that drunken teamster. I thought you — well, that you just weren't the romantic kind."

The surprise of that held Ransome speechless for a moment. And it made him a trifle ashamed. In this hushed interval, while he read what her eyes were frankly revealing, Ransome understood that she was offering more than a ranch partnership; she was offering him the warmth and affection a woman could give a man. And she would give it gladly, generously. . . .

But because Belle Gillum personified the wondrous, flame-fashioned image of his campfire dreams, Ransome slowly shook his head. Even though he would never hold Belle in his arms again, he couldn't forget the wild sweet flavor of her lips, nor the gentle flare of her nostrils when she smiled, nor the way she had whispered his name just before he kissed her.

He was thinking about that, and cursing himself for a witless fool when he limped into a room at the Union Hotel. Just before he went to sleep, Ransome remembered Fay's parting words; how she'd stood there in the doorway and peered up at him and said in a queerly puzzled voice, "You act like you're the one that died tonight instead of Cameo."

CHAPTER 18

A Personal Thing

It was nearly noon when Lee Ransome awoke. Washing at the bureau he eyed himself in its fly-specked mirror and thought: *I need a shave and a haircut.* But he needed food more, and so he went directly to the dining room.

There were half a dozen customers already eating. Ransome noticed that they peered at him with more than passing interest; he was wondering about that when the waitress asked, "Are you the one that killed all those men at Gunman's Camp last night?"

So that was it. That was why they were all gawking at him as if he were some kind of two-headed freak. As this flirty-eyed waitress was looking at him now. . . .

"I came here to eat, not to gossip," he said gruffly.

"Well, you might be interested to know the coroner is looking for you," she announced in high-headed resentment. "And so are others."

Ransome grunted and ate his meal in frowning silence, ignoring the inquisitive glances that focused on him from surrounding tables. It was all familiar, this curious staring and low-voiced mumbling from bystanders. They'd acted the same way after shootouts in Texas Junction, looking at him with curious, unfriendly eyes. It didn't occur to them that a gunhawk lawman had feelings, as anyone else. They seemed to think he was just a lawenforcement machine incapable of fear or regret or a need to be as other men.

To hell with them, Ransome thought, paying his bill. Let the silly sons look their fill; let them gawk their goddam eyes out. . . .

Remembering the displeasure he had glimpsed in Belle Gillum's eyes when he took Society Slim's gun, Ransome muttered, "To hell with her also."

A man could take only so much. He had taken aplenty since the day he rode into Concho Basin. And lost aplenty. He had owned a good horse and saddle and camp outfit; and considerable more blood than he had in him now. He was leaving empty handed, empty inside and out. But he'd got the job done, by God. Even though it hadn't gone the way he wanted, the deal was finished.

That was what this tall, shaggy-haired Texan was thinking as he limped out to the hotel veranda on his way to the stage depot. And the bitterness of that thinking was mirrored in his bleak gray eyes. He peered straight ahead, not wanting to see the inevitable faces that would be watching, and so didn't notice Belle Gillum who sat on the veranda bench, until she spoke his name. . . .

Ransome took another step, as if not hearing her. Then he turned his head and stared in wide-eyed astonishment and said, "You?"

She nodded, and for a queerly suspended interval they just stood there looking at each other. Then she motioned for him to sit beside her, saying, "I've been waiting almost an hour."

Ransome sat down, so completely puzzled by her presence here that he didn't know what to say, and so said nothing.

"Pat Grogan told me you are leaving on the one o'clock stage," Belle announced.

"Yeah," Ransome said.

"Why are you leaving so soon?"

"Didn't see no reason for staying," Ransome explained soberly. "That deal at Gunman's Camp went haywire. Too damned much shooting, and too much killing. No way to prove my story about Kimble without witnesses to what he said."

"What made you so sure I wouldn't believe you?" Belle asked censuringly. Then, not waiting for a reply, she said, "You'll be glad to know Sheriff Baffert didn't die."

That news jolted Ransome into utter confusion. "You don't know what you're talking about," he insisted. "Tate Tarborrow lit a match and looked at him and told me Baffert was shot through the head. He wouldn't mistake the sheriff for somebody else."

"The bullet dug a piece of hide off Sid's forehead, and gave him a concussion," Belle explained. "Sid was staggering around in a daze when Pat Grogan got to Gunman's Camp. But he's all right now, except for a bad headache. And he told me the things he heard Cameo Kimble tell at the supper table last night." She grimaced, adding in a self-accusing voice, "How could he have fooled me so?"

Haltingly, in the fashion of a man counting an unexpected windfall and astonished by it, Ransome said, "Baffert heard everything Kimble said. That means Jim Tarborrow gets out of Yuma Prison within one week's time, perhaps sooner. There'll be no more fighting, and no more trouble for Luke Beauford. Tom Rynning gets everything he wanted."

"It's wonderful, isn't it," Belle agreed smilingly. She got up, saying, "I must get back to take care of Dad. He's much better, but he has to be watched. I just wanted to — to tell you how much we all appreciate what you've done for us, Lee."

Ransome stood up, fingering his hat and not knowing how to explain why he was no longer in a hurry to leave Concho Basin. . . .

"Charity asked me to say good-bye for her," Belle reported. "She says you can have any one of her chickens you want. And Kid Beauford says he'd appreciate you putting in a good word for him with Captain Rynning. He wants to be an Arizona Ranger, like you."

"He can take my place," Ransome said. "I'm through wearing any kind of badge."

Still holding his hat in hand, he walked along the veranda with her. He said, "There's something I'd like to tell you, but I can't say it here, with all these people gawking at us. It wouldn't be fitting."

"If you've got time you could ride up the road a little way with me in the wagon," Belle suggested and smiled at him, so that her nostrils flared gently.

"Sure," Ransome said, taking her arm. "I've got plenty of time."

"Is it something personal?" Belle asked as they walked toward Grogan's Livery.

Ransome nodded. "The most personal thing a man can say to a woman."

And now, because she was a magnet strongly pulling him, Ransome asked, "Would you marry a man like me, Belle?"

She looked up at him, meeting his questing gaze with a kindred questing. "I'd like to marry a man exactly like you," she said, and when he took her in his arms, she asked, "Do you think this is fitting — out here in public?"

But her lips were there for him and so Ransome told her what he thought without the use of words. . . .

The employees of Thorndike Press hope you have enjoyed this Large Print book. All our Thorndike and Wheeler Large Print titles are designed for easy reading, and all our books are made to last. Other Thorndike Press Large Print books are available at your library, through selected bookstores, or directly from us.

For information about titles, please call:

(800) 223-1244

or visit our Web site at:

www.gale.com/thorndike
www.gale.com/wheeler

To share your comments, please write:

Publisher
Thorndike Press
295 Kennedy Memorial Drive
Waterville, ME   04901